NOBODY'S GHOST

CHRIS COOPER

DREADFUL
MEDIA

Nobody's Ghost

Published by Dreadful Media

Enjoy the book? Please consider leaving a review at goodreads.com or amazon.com. Every review helps. To receive news of new publications, events, and exclusive offers, please sign up for the Dreadful Media Newsletter on our website. WWW.DREADFULMEDIA.COM

SPECIAL THANKS

Olivia Arscott
Dave Cutler
Aimee Futcher
Aunt Kim
Juliana T. Johnson
Jacob & Taylor Mathers
Rockelle & Tanner Reynolds
Carlos Arturo Soto
Jenni D Strand

"Welcome to the Blumfeld Hatchet House." I put on my fake tour-guide grin and made a sweeping gesture toward the three-story Queen Anne-style home behind me. She stood in austere beauty, with a large turret mounted on her left side and a wraparound porch spanning her right. The previous owners had painted the siding a putrid pus-yellow, which I hated but was too cheap to do anything about.

"How many of you know the story of Henry Blumfeld and his hatchet?" I asked the group.

Three-quarters of them raised their hands.

"And how many of you were dragged here by a friend?"

That got the rest.

"Well, regardless of what brought you here, you're all in for a treat."

I guided the group up the front steps, past the unkempt bushes that added to the house's creepy look. One of the porch boards crackled under my feet. I needed to fix it before one of my more robust customers crashed through the porch and slapped me with a million-dollar lawsuit.

"In 1923, after a long day at the office, Henry Blumfeld returned home with a box of his personal office belongings tucked under his arm."

Once inside, we turned right into the living room, and I pointed at an old leather chair sitting next to an antique record player. "He set the box next to his armchair, poured a glass of one of his finest whiskeys, and put on his favorite record while his wife made dinner in the kitchen. After a glass or two or three, something in Henry snapped. He ventured to the side of the house, pulled a hatchet from the old tree stump next to the woodpile, and strolled into the kitchen."

We passed through the dining room and into the kitchen. I approached the farmhouse sink, which was bordered by two ceiling-height cabinets and a large window that looked out to the backyard.

"Not sure if it was the whiskey, poor aim, or a change of heart, but his first strike missed his lovely wife completely." I ran my finger along a narrow gash in the butcher-block countertop. "Fortunately for Mrs. Blumfeld, Henry's hatchet hit hard, wedging itself deeply enough to get stuck. Just imagine, you're cooking dinner for your family, and *wham!*" I slammed my hand down on the counter, causing several in the group to jump. "You turn your head and see your husband standing next to you, trying to free a hatchet from the place your hand had rested just moments ago."

I gestured for the group to follow me back to the entryway then wrapped my hand around the staircase railing that wound to the second floor. "As Henry tried to free his hatchet, Mrs. Blumfeld raced upstairs to save the children. Unfortunately for them all, Henry was waiting for them on the landing when they returned, hatchet in hand. Mrs. Blumfeld retreated to one of her daughter's bedrooms, tucked her children into a crawl space, then returned to the hallway to confront her husband as he reached the second floor."

The wooden steps creaked under our feet as the tour group climbed the stairs.

"His first strike caught her in the forearm. She fell against the banister as Henry raised his hatchet once more but dodged the second blow, scrambled to her feet, and ran screaming to the master bedroom."

I guided them to the door at the end of the hallway, twisted the glass knob, and pulled. "If you look there," I said, pointing at a spot in the hardwood at the foot of the bed, "you'll see the bloodstain marking Mrs. Blumfeld's final resting place. Lizzie Borden may have given her mother forty whacks, but Henry left such a mess, the police couldn't count. Later owners have tried to refinish the floors, but the stain reappears every time."

"It looks wet," a man said from the back of the group.

I knelt and ran my hand over the spot, coating my palm in a layer of sticky red liquid. I pulled my hand away and held it up to show them. "It's never done that before. If you'll excuse me, I'm going to run to the restroom and wash this off."

"Corn syrup," I heard someone say as I turned the corner to the bathroom. As I scrubbed, several heavy thuds came from the bedroom where Mrs. Blumfeld had taken her final breaths, followed by a piercing scream.

I rushed back into the bedroom. "What happened?"

Two women wearing sweatshirts from the local university stood over a set of candlesticks lying on the hardwood floor.

"They just fell over," the short brunette said.

"Mrs. Blumfeld has been known to make a mess up here," I replied casually. "Let's continue the tour, and I'll clean this up later."

I returned to the hallway. "She's just reminding you to be wary of her husband, or perhaps she's pleading for you to save her children. Speaking of children, little Helen and Robert normally slept in that room down the hall, but all three hid in Virginia's room that afternoon."

I led them to the bedroom next door. Sunlight cast a cheery glow over the room as it beamed in from the large window bordered with floral curtains. A cross-stitched alphabet hung above a tiled fireplace, and a child-size dining table sat in the middle of the room on top of a decorative rug.

"If you look at the far end of the room, next to the bed, you'll see a little door leading to a storage space. Mrs. Blumfeld packed all three children inside, and there they hid as Henry paced through the house, brandishing his hatchet, wishing to bid his darlings one final goodnight. Perhaps one of them sneezed, coughed, or screamed. Whatever happened, Henry eventually found them. Please, have a look around, but I ask that you not touch anything. Most items were in this very room on that fateful day."

As the group dispersed, the two college women went straight for the door to the storage space.

"I'll give you five bucks if you crawl in there," the brunette said to the tall blonde.

"No way. You do it."

"Give me ten, and I will. All this stuff is made up anyway."

"Fine."

The brunette turned toward me.

"Go ahead," I said, gesturing toward the door. As she crouched down to turn the tiny brass handle, I addressed the rest of the group. "Folks, I believe we have someone who would like to try the crawl space."

"Cold day in hell before I'd do that," said a man whose wife looked equally frightened. I hadn't gotten their names, but I'd dubbed them Beer Gut and Bad Perm in my head. When I started these tours, I'd tried to learn every-one's name but found it better not to personalize them—I felt less guilty later.

"No reason to be afraid. I've done hundreds of tours. A dozen people have tried the crawl space, and not a single person has been maimed or physically scarred." I grinned. "Psychological scars are a different story."

The crawl space tours were my favorite, and even if a murderous hatchet-wielding ghost were to suck them into the underworld, they'd all signed waivers beforehand.

"Just be warned, some claim to have heard whispering children inside," I said.

"What did they say?" the brunette asked.

"He's coming. He's coming," I whispered.

That was too much for Bad Perm, who stepped away and peered out the window on the far side of the room.

"It's not real," Beer Gut said as he rubbed his wife's shoulders. "The whole thing is just an act. You know ghosts aren't real."

"I want to go," she said under her breath.

"You promised to do this with me," he shot back.

Bad Perm turned and leaned against the window. "I'll watch from here."

I waved the brunette on as she jerked the door handle. The door held firm.

"That door swells," I said. "Sometimes you have to give it a good yank."

She pulled hard, and the door flung open, letting out a plume of musty attic air.

The brunette looked into the darkness, and her hand trembled as she grabbed the frame of the door and pulled herself inside.

"I have to admit, I've kept something from you," I said. "I led you to believe that Henry murdered his children like he'd murdered his wife, but that wasn't the case. Henry found all three children hiding in the crawl space but didn't kill them. He let time finish them off. Henry flipped the lock on the door, pushed this very bed against it, and left all three to bake in the summer heat."

I knelt and ran my fingers along the inside of the door. "If you look closely, you can still see the fingernail scratches."

"That's disgusting," the brunette said from inside the crawl space. "I'm getting out of here."

"Let me get your picture first," her friend replied.

I backed away as she lifted her camera to take a photo of the woman inside.

As the girl posed inside the crawl space, the door slammed shut, and she let out a terrified scream.

"Jesus Christ!" Bad Perm yelled from behind me.

The brunette's friend gripped the small brass door handle, but the crawl space door refused to budge.

"Let me," I said as the screaming continued from the other side.

Beer Gut and Bad Perm were already plodding down the stairs. They'd made it to the entryway by the time I pulled the girl out of the crawl space. The rest of the group waited in terror.

"Are you all right?" I asked.

"I want to go," she panted.

"But we're not—"

"Now!" she screamed.

A record player scratched from the first floor, and Bad Perm let out an inhuman scream as tinny music filled the air.

I corralled the rest of the group down the steps toward the front door and arrived just in time to see Bad Perm hit the floor.

Beer Gut pointed to the sitting room. "It just started playing." His voice wavered as he bent over to help his wife to her feet.

"The ghosts are lively today," I said as I led the group into the sitting room to see the record player.

As they rounded the corner, the kitchen cabinets flew open, and dishes cascaded to the floor, sending shards of floral-patterned ceramic across the kitchen and into the dining room. As the group stood in horror, the dining room table levitated.

"This isn't normal. They're angry!" I shouted. "Run!"

Bad Perm had barely regained her footing as Beer Gut dragged her toward the door. The rest of the group fled down the walkway to the street.

"And don't forget to leave a review on Trip Advisor!" I shouted after them.

I turned toward the mess waiting for me inside. "Welp, time to get to work."

Henry always made such a mess, but it was great for business. Henry's tale had one major problem, though—I'd made the whole thing up.

CHAPTER TWO

I haunted Hatchet House. Well, I used the term "haunt" loosely. I wasn't a ghost and never intended to be one, but since my early teens, I'd been able to move objects with my mind. While most boys my age had gotten acne, I'd come down with a severe case of telekinesis.

A kid named Chubs—I'll let you guess why—had pinned me against a brick wall. As he cocked his fist to sock me in the eye, I noticed a basketball sitting dead center in a hopscotch square, until suddenly it wasn't. The ball hung in midair, unbeknownst to Chubs, and propelled itself into the back of his pudgy head. Chubs let go of my collar and turned to face his attacker but found no one behind him. Somehow, I had wished for the ball to attack, and the ball had obliged.

Flash forward a few years, and I'd honed my gift into a moneymaking craft.

I swept the broken china into a pile on the floor and unlocked the storage closet where I kept spare sets. All the silverware on the dining table were antiques, but the dishes that flew from the cupboards were cheap sets from the local discount store. No one seemed to notice the Made in China stamps on the plates as they came flying toward them. I had probably gone through a thousand sets since I'd started haunting the place three years prior.

I may have been raking in the dough lately, but I'd barely had enough to buy the house in the first place. A mortgage was a no-go—my credit was shit—so I'd started looking at property auctions. I was still unsure how I'd pulled off buying Hatchet House, but being in the right place at the right time and finding a desperate owner had helped. Once I'd patched the roof and it stopped raining inside of the place, I'd gotten to work assembling its history.

The Villisca Axe Murder House inspired the story line. I added the bloody spot after reading a blog post about a haunting at an asylum in Ohio. I pulled bits from hauntings here and there until I'd created a patchwork tale that even had some of the locals convinced.

The hatchet mark in the counter was authentic. I had made it myself with an old axe I'd found in the garage.

The tour wasn't always the same. Whenever I grew bored, I would add a new element, like the wet blood patch. I tried to keep the story consistent, just in case anyone scrutinized it, and I'd even placed a few bread crumbs online to give the story more merit.

Sure, there had been skeptics—armchair researchers who could find no evidence that Henry nor his family had ever existed—but after a visit to Hatchet House, no one cared what the records said. Most came for the thrill, not the historical accuracy. When asked about details, I chalked the inconsistencies up to conspiracy. Perhaps a few powerful voices in the neighborhood had connections and had made the whole story go away because no one would want to buy a house next to an axe murderer. A fire in the early 1930s had wiped out the local property records, so keeping the lie under wraps wasn't difficult.

The tours had taken off after a national ghost hunter show featured the house and Henry's story. I'd gotten a call from a producer who'd asked if the team could come in, take some readings, and spend the weekend. I'd agreed so long as I could stay with them. Telekinesis worked like a radio—if I was nearby, I could control most objects in the house, but the signal grew weaker as I moved farther away.

The ghost-hunting idiots poked around with heat-sensing cameras and microphones, picking up mysterious floating orbs and cold spots along the way. I had to do very little work to convince them the place was haunted. One of their microphones caught a conversation from a few passersby, and that nearly had them convinced. I couldn't play the blood-patch trick since I made the stuff with corn syrup and food coloring, and I tried not to repeat any of the obvious gags people might recognize on the tour, but a few slamming doors were enough to get the job done. They found no strings, hidden receivers, or other signs of trickery because none existed.

After the show aired, people flocked to the house, and I ended up with a six-month waiting list for tours the second year. Sometimes I felt guilty for scaring people, especially those who ran screaming from the place, but I reminded myself that I was simply giving them what they'd paid for.

Although I surrounded myself with macabre stories and haunted tales, I didn't believe any of it. Still, as long as those stories paid my bills, I would play the part of the frightened tour guide. At twenty-five bucks a pop and two tours each day, I was raking in the dough. If my new plan panned out, I would be able to move out of my haunted hellhole and buy a nice house with cold, hard cash. Not bad for a high school dropout.

The ghost hunter show had taught me that exposure was key. Most tour takers didn't care whether the story or experiences were legit. They just wanted the thrill of the scare. If that small network show had given me such a boost, a spot on a major network would change my life, so I sent feelers to a handful of shows on larger stations. I hadn't heard anything yet, but I was optimistic.

By the time I'd cleared the broken dishes, the sun had

slunk halfway behind the horizon, casting a warm orange glow over the neighborhood.

I grabbed my jacket from the hall closet, locked the place up, and took my early-evening stroll to the bar down the street, reveling in the cool weather and the smell of decaying autumn leaves.

The bar sat a few blocks from Hatchet House and had been my favorite haunt since I'd moved to town. I'd spent many a night wandering home from the place. At least, I assumed I had walked and hadn't been carried. I was typically too plastered to remember.

The wooden barstool legs ground against the tile as I perched on top of the cracked leather cushion and scooted up to the bar. I leaned against the counter and rested my feet on the pole that ran along the floor.

The bartender turned toward me. "The usual?" he asked with a smile.

I nodded and pulled my wallet from the pocket of my frayed jeans.

"You know, I'd let you sit here for free." He tugged the dishrag from his back pocket, wiped the counter, and laid down a fresh napkin.

"Just need the smell," I replied. "Part of the ritual. The view's nice too." I gave him a cheesy wink.

He chuckled and turned to grab a bottle from the backlit liquor shelf.

"One year today," I said.

He set two shot glasses in front of me. "You're a masochist, aren't you? An alcoholic who surrounds himself with booze but refuses to drink. What kind of hell is that?" He poured a shot for me and one for himself before pushing the glass toward me. "I'm sure they'd frown on this in AA."

"They don't need to know." I tipped my glass in his direction. "Cheers."

He sucked the shot down as smoothly as only a hot, tattooed bartender could, while I settled for a nostril-burning whiff. *Never drink, only smell.* It was the deal I'd made with myself. I got to keep the ambiance of the bar without the soul-sucking addiction.

Truthfully, I didn't come for the ambiance, at least not anymore. I'd spent many hours in that hole-in-the-wall gay bar, and the only good thing to come from it was my relationship with the bartender, Patrick.

His smile was disarming, even under the harsh overhead bar lights, and he kept a perfectly sculpted five o'clock shadow. Even though his eyes always looked tired under his yellow tortoiseshell frames, he exuded playfulness. I could tell he was compensating for something, masking his experiences, but that was the great part about our relationship—he didn't like to talk about the past, and neither did I. We were perfect for each other.

At first, I'd figured he would probably treat me like everyone else. After all, Patrick's job was to be friendly, but he could have barred me for life after I'd pissed on the corner of the bar on an unusually rowdy evening. Instead, he slipped the info for a local AA group into my jacket pocket while I was busy heaving in the bathroom. Then he called a cab. If that wasn't friendship, I didn't know what was.

I'd been sober a month before I wandered back in. I showed him my red chip and thanked him. In one of my uncharacteristically suave moves, I offered to buy him dinner to make amends. I figured if he turned me down, I wouldn't be back to the bar anyway. But to my surprise, he'd said yes.

"Drink's on the house," he said. "One year's something to be proud of."

I shook my head and pulled a card from my wallet. "Gotta support the small-business community."

"Suit yourself."

When he returned with my card, he lingered a bit longer than usual. "Congrats," he said, handing it back with the tattooed arm I'd grown so fond of over our dysfunctional years together. Black tree roots ran out from under his rolled flannel sleeve.

"Up to anything tonight?" I asked.

"You're looking at it," he replied. "I'll be here 'til close and then some."

"What about tomorrow? Maybe we could grab dinner?"

He grinned. "I'd love to, but tomorrow's the big drag show. I won't be out until three or four."

I knew an alcoholic spending so much time at a bar was pretty messed up, but Patrick and I already had enough trouble seeing each other on opposite schedules, and God, I liked him. He was kind, a bit of a hipster, and had a hell of a body underneath that flannel shirt. The urge to drink never went away, but it seemed to dwindle whenever we were together, even if we were surrounded by bottles of the stuff that had gotten me into so much trouble to begin with.

I'd made a few loose acquaintances in town—the local shop owners and a neighbor or two—but running the tours and keeping the house in shape was all-consuming. As soon as things became manageable, a pipe would burst or a family of raccoons would take up residence in the attic. Life had been lonely before Patrick.

I hung out at the bar for an hour or so—the place was dead, so we got to talk more than usual—then wandered my way back to Hatchet House.

Once inside, I pulled the skeleton key from my pocket and unlocked the door to Helen and Robert's room. Helen and Robert were also figments of my imagination, and their fake room served as my real-life apartment. I kept it locked during the tours, and whenever guests would request to see it, I would say it was in disrepair.

I'd fit a mini fridge and microwave in the corner next to

a small TV with a set of rabbit ears. The twin bed was too small, and my feet hung over the edge, but it was free, and anything larger would have taken up the entire room. I kept most of my personal stuff tucked in that tiny bedroom. Nothing ruined creepy ambiance like dirty laundry and a stack of old take-out containers.

I'd lived in the house long enough to fill a small book-shelf on the far wall with horror novels and research for the business.

I flipped the TV to one of the three channels I could get with the antenna and popped a frozen meal into the microwave. Wavy lines scrolled across the screen as some schlub sat on the couch while his unreasonably attractive wife nagged him about housecleaning. If I added a few empties on the table, subtracted the humor, and threw in a few slaps for good measure, I would have been watching my childhood unfold on screen. But nobody wanted realism in their sitcoms.

I must have dozed off when the shrill ring of the house phone pulled me from a shallow slumber.

"Hatchet House Murder Tours," I slurred as I wiped the drool from the corner of my mouth.

"Hello, I'm trying to reach Clifford Morris," a woman said on the other end.

I hated the sound of my name. Clifford was a family name. My older sister had the good fortune to come out female, so my parents blessed me with Clifford and the history of rampant alcoholism that came with it.

"That's me," I said with a forced smile as if it made a difference to the person on the other end.

"Hi, Clifford. My name's Valerie, and I'm calling on behalf of Delilah Rhodes."

The name rang a bell, but I couldn't place it at first.

"I'm sorry," I replied. "The name sounds familiar, but—"

"She's the preeminent psychic of daytime television," she said as if she'd said that same line a thousand times before.

Click. I'd seen Delilah on TV a few times, and her production company had been on my email list. From what I could remember, she was a pencil-thin blonde in a no-nonsense pantsuit who did cold readings in front of an audience. A scammer for sure, although who was I to judge?

"We got your message. We're working on a new documentary series on haunted places and are looking for candidates for the show. We think Hatchet House might be a great fit."

Free publicity! The thought scrolled across my head like a news ticker.

"For her daytime show?" I asked.

Valerie waffled. "Not exactly. I can't tell you which

streaming service we're filming for, but let's just say it has north of one hundred million subscribers."

The receiver slipped from my hand, and I scrambled to catch it before it hit the ground. I would be able to triple the tour fee with that sort of publicity.

"What exactly are you looking for?" I asked.

"We'd send our production team out to Hatchet House and shoot for a day or two. You'd just have to let us poke around a bit, and Delilah would also do an interview with you."

"Kind of like *Ghost Explorers International*?" I asked. "They did a show on Hatchet House a few years ago."

Valerie laughed. "Just don't say that in front of Delilah if you want your show to see the light of day. What Delilah does is different... real."

Sure. That's what everyone says.

"And we would pay you for any expenses incurred from filming."

"When can you be here?" I asked.

"So you're interested?"

"Absolutely!"

"Great. Let me check in with the team, and we'll get back to you with details and all the paperwork. We'll be in touch."

The phone clicked on the other end.

CHAPTER THREE

The week before the production crew arrived, I got to work. Some typical scares would be too risky to pull in front of discerning eyes. If Delilah was a con artist, she would easily be able to spot another, so I would have to depend on my magical invisible grip as I had with the ghost-hunter goons.

I cleared the house of the stacks of extra china, spare hatchets, and squeeze bottles of fake blood and locked them in the storage shed. I scrubbed the bloody spot clean of any remnants of fake blood, but the stain remained thanks to water damage from the leaky roof I'd since repaired.

The production crew arrived a few hours before Delilah to take preliminary shots and scope out the place. A white van pulled up in front of the house just as I'd finished mowing the grass, and a woman emerged from the passenger side. Her long red hair curled slightly at the ends as it rested against her leather jacket. She was a few inches taller than me and looked as if she were a former athlete.

"Clifford?" she asked.

"Cliff is fine," I replied.

She stuck out her hand. "I'm Valerie—Val. Nice to meet you." She looked up at the house. "What a beautiful place. Crazy how so much beauty can hide such an evil history."

I smiled. "Just glad we can shed some light on what happened here to honor the family's memory."

"Tony and Jay will get the equipment set up, and we'll take a look around. Delilah will be here in a few for the interview."

"I'm surprised she can take a break from her talk show to fly all the way out here," I said.

"They're prerecorded for the rest of the week," Val replied. "She'd get nothing done if she filmed a show every day."

"Oh."

Val's crew had a different vibe than the *Ghost Explorer* baboons. Val was professional and organized, as were her crew members. They moved from room to room, snapping pictures and mapping out filming angles, but no one mentioned cold chills or floating orbs in the camera.

"Not going to take temperature readings?" I asked.

Val laughed. "We don't need gimmicks."

I wondered if I'd gotten myself in over my head.

After the crew finished planning the shoot, Jay brought me over to the dining room table, where he'd set a black box filled with makeup. Jay was a heavyset Italian with a jet-black mustache and curly hair that bounced against his shoulders as he walked. He wore a Hawaiian shirt, khaki shorts, sandals, and was the oddest-looking makeup artist I'd ever seen.

"How long have you been doing makeup?" I asked.

Jay chuckled as he brushed foundation on my cheek. "A few years. Val likes to run with a small crew, and our budget's pretty tight. Means we have to wear a lot of different hats."

"How did you get the makeup job?"

"Used to do makeup for horror movies. Budgets were slim, so I had to do the creatures and the babes. This isn't much of a stretch."

"And which one am I?" I asked straight-faced.

"I'll let you guess," he shot back.

"Any movies I'd recognize?"

"No. That's why I'm powdering your ugly mug, Jack." He grinned wide, revealing a set of luminescent white teeth that seemed too big for his mouth. He chomped on a toothpick as he finished with the brush.

"She's here," Val said. "Let's set up for the first introductions."

"You're good to go," Jay said. "Only so much I can do

with a face like that." He chuckled. I couldn't tell whether he was joking, but I could only take a guy in a Hawaiian shirt so seriously.

I stepped toward the front window and looked out onto the street. Delilah's driver had parked a Rolls-Royce in front of the production van and helped her out of the car. She chatted away on her cell phone and said a few words to the driver, who climbed back inside and cut the engine.

Shoestring budget, my ass.

Val went out to meet her and waited patiently for her to finish the phone call.

Delilah removed her sunglasses, handed them to Val, and turned toward the house. The blue collar of her dress shirt was perfectly starched and hung stiffly over the neck of her beige suit jacket. The sunlight caught the slick surface of her polished heels. Her eyes scanned the house until they reached the window where I stood staring like a freshly powdered idiot. I smiled, and she furrowed her brow at first then returned my smile half-heartedly.

She paused in the walkway and straightened her collar as Val opened the front door.

"We're ready," Val said.

"What do I do?" I asked.

Jay laughed from behind the camera.

"Just answer the door," Val replied.

Tony lifted the second camera as Val stepped out of the shot and closed the door behind her.

When the doorbell rang, I stepped awkwardly toward the door. My effort to act naturally made my movements anything but natural. The camera lenses seemed to have sucked the confidence from my body, and my stomach went sour. I twisted the knob and opened the door as Delilah stood waiting on the other side.

"Hello," I said with far too much energy.

After an awkward introduction, Delilah asked for a quick tour. We went from room to room as I told the story I'd rehearsed so many times before. I wanted to get a feel for her before I tried any tricks, but I had plenty ready at a moment's notice.

I guessed all scam artists had to be intelligent, but Delilah was especially sharp.

"I've checked the records in the area," she said. "I couldn't find anything about a Henry Blumfeld."

I was prepared for that. "You've probably seen an article or two about the fire, then. It wiped out the city archives and property records."

I started with the record player, an oldie but a goody. The crew jumped as sound crept through the speakers, but Delilah remained calm and composed. She examined the player for any signs of tampering then, having found none, made a note on her memo pad and continued on her way.

The slamming door to the crawl space left her equally

unfazed, although Tony, who was a third of Jay's size, was visibly sweating as he crawled back out with the hand-held camera. I showed him the fingernail marks I had refreshed with a Dremel, and he looked as if he might vomit.

The hatchet in the back door was a new trick, and it took concentration to aim it at the door while sitting in the living room. I'd practiced with an axe handle a few times from different points in the house, and aside from the time I'd nearly broken a window, I'd gotten good enough to use the real thing.

Delilah ran her finger along the handle and pried it loose from the door, with the camera crew tracking her closely.

I shook floorboards, tossed candlesticks, and slammed doors, but Delilah simply moved from one incident to the next without so much as a word or a hair out of place on her perfectly primped head. Eventually, she tucked her notebook into a pocket and stopped taking notes altogether.

"Can we sit and chat?" she asked as we stood in the dining room while the rest of the crew returned from recording the chaos in the kitchen.

"Sure," I replied.

She turned toward Val and whispered, then Val motioned for Jay and Tony to put down the camera gear.

"Don't you want to record this?" I asked.

"No need," Delilah replied coldly as she pulled out a dining room chair for herself.

We sat at the table, and Delilah leaned in close. "If all the Blumfeld records were wiped in the fire, how did you find out about them?"

"The old owner," I lied. "But I could point you to some online articles."

"Flimsy blogs and posts on a few online forums are hardly compelling. Most legitimate articles refer to the tour and use you as the only point of reference for the story."

"I—"

"Do you think I'm a fool?" she asked. "A fraud?"

I could feel the blood rush to my cheeks as I tried to reassure myself that I'd thoroughly covered my tracks. The house was free of wires, fake blood, and any other signs of deception. "No, not at all. Why would I think that?" I sat back in my chair as my heart raced. The queasy feeling from earlier came back in full force. The pre-tour microwave burritos had been a bad idea.

She leaned back and put her finger to her lips. "There are no spirits here."

"What do you mean?"

"Haunted places have an aura. I've checked the place from top to bottom, and it's spiritually vacant."

"I assure you, it's haunted," I replied, my voice wavering.

She leaned in again. "I've met people like you before.

You'll do anything for your fifteen minutes or to make a buck. Tell me, how do you sleep at night?"

"Excuse me?"

Her eyes stared right through me as if my soul were bare for her to see. "We're done here. Pack up the gear," she said as she looked over at Val.

I saw my fortune following her as she rose from her chair.

"Wait." I reached over the table and grabbed her hand as she turned to leave the room.

A surge of electricity shot through me, and I slid out of my chair onto the floor, smacking my forehead on the edge of the table as I fell.

When I came to, Tony stood over me while Val helped Delilah to her feet and back into a dining room chair.

I pulled myself up as Delilah stared at me with a look of disgust.

"I'm so sorry," I said. "I don't know what happ—"

"Come home, Cliff," she replied in a voice that was an octave lower than normal.

"What?" I asked.

She lowered her head and twitched as her fingers pulsed on the table. She murmured, but I couldn't make out the words.

"I can't understand you."

"It's time to come home, Cliff." She raised her head, revealing her sickening smile and curled lips. Her pupils were wide, the black obscuring any signs of the colored irises. "Come home and face what you've done." Her head cocked to the side, and her eyes rolled back until only the whites were visible. She screamed and fell limp to the floor.

The air pulsed around me, and an odd static cling caused the hair on my arms to stand on end.

"Jesus Christ!" Jay said. "What kind of voodoo shit was that?"

Val rushed toward the crumpled woman as I sat in shock at the dining room table.

"Delilah." Val tapped her lightly on the cheek. "Get some water," she snapped at me.

I ran to the sink and grabbed a glass from the cupboard. When I returned, Delilah was staring at the ceiling with a vacant gaze.

"I'm okay," she murmured. Her eyes darted from side to side then came to rest as she locked them with mine. "We're leaving."

The rest of the crew looked legitimately terrified.

"Has that happened before?" I asked.

Jay shook his head, causing his toothpick to fall from his gaping mouth.

Delilah scooted against the wall and massaged her temples. "Pack up the gear."

As Val helped Delilah to her feet, I stepped toward her. "Wait." I reached for her once again.

"Don't touch me!" she screamed, sliding along the wall toward the door.

I chased after her. "Just tell me what happened."

She spun around. "You're a fraud for one. There are no ghosts haunting this house except for the ones you've created. But something evil's following you, Cliff, and has been for a long time. I don't know how or what, but I can't help you." She slammed the front door behind her.

The statement sent chills up my spine. "This is just part of the show, right?" I asked Val.

She shook her head. "Afraid not."

"I've seen some spooky shit, but nothing like that," Jay added.

Val pulled out her phone. "This will set us back." She looked up at Jay and Tony. "You heard her. Let's get this shit packed up and into the van. Maybe we can bump up that taping in Massachusetts."

"You can't just leave. What about the show?"

She gestured for the other two to get going. "Sorry, Cliff. We've got to call it."

The crew had packed up completely and left within the hour, and I stood in disbelief as the van pulled away, carrying my fortune with it.

I was screwed. I didn't know how Delilah had figured out everything was a hoax, but one news article, and I would be out of business. *And what the hell was the exorcist act about?*

I ran the day over in my head as I lay in bed later that night. I tried to stop the racing thoughts and the worry, but they persisted. A drink or two would have taken care of them. I was thirsty like I hadn't been in some time.

Maybe the whole thing was some joke. Maybe it was fodder for Delilah's new show. But the cameras hadn't even been rolling.

CHAPTER FOUR

Hard, uneven lumps pressed into my body, and I opened my eyes as the wind blew a puff of dirt up my nose. I pushed myself up, and pieces of gravel embedded themselves into my palms as the blacktop singed my skin. I brushed off the rocks as the world around me came into focus. I stood in the middle of a two-lane road lined on one side by blooming magnolia trees and the other by a rickety wooden fence.

"Faggot!" The word hit me harder than the stone that followed. I grabbed the back of my head and scrambled as several more rocks flew in my direction.

I recognized my surroundings and turned to face my rock-wielding adversaries. I'd worked hard to wipe Chubs from my memory, but somehow the overgrown mutant asshole kept making appearances. Two goons stood on either side of him.

"What's your problem?" I shot back. I tried to puff up my chest, but they saw right through the act.

Chubs snarled as his fist clung tightly to another rock. He cocked his arm to fire again.

I looked to my left and noticed a dirt path blocked off by a flimsy metal gate held closed by a rusty chain. I didn't wait for Chubs to answer and darted toward it.

"Get him!" I heard from behind.

I scaled the gate, my heart pounding in my chest, and looked back. The trio was forced to leave their bikes behind.

I knew I could outrun them, or at least I could outrun Chubs. I may not have been the poster child for physical fitness, but Chubs had a Twinkie in his gullet half the time and wheezed standing still. I sprinted over the creek bridge as the gang's sneakers pounded into the dirt behind me. Somehow, even though I was running as fast as I could, the trio closed in.

"Come on, Chubs. We can't go up to the crazy Duncans'," one boy panted. "That place is haunted."

The Duncan Plantation sat framed by an oak-lined drive, decaying from decades of neglect. Thin wooden columns held up the two-story roof that had been spotted with thick green patches of algae and moss, and several shingles protruded at odd angles like loose baby teeth.

I tripped over a fallen branch and fell face first into the dirt. *Shit, shit, shit.* I was dead meat.

"Hold him down," Chubs said.

The other two pinned my arms to the ground. I'd bitten my lip on the way down, and the taste of copper filled my mouth.

Chubs walked to the edge of the path and yanked a broken branch free from a tangle of vines. "I'll teach you to run," he said as he centered himself over me and lifted the branch above his head.

The other boys were pressing me down so hard I couldn't breathe, and my eyes stung as dirt blurred my vision.

Chubs smirked when he saw the tears forming in the corners of my eyes. "You really are a fairy, aren't you? No wonder your mom ran out on you." His sinister smile was dingy yellow as if he'd never seen a toothbrush before.

I exhaled as the world went quiet around me. Chubs swung down with the branch, and I closed my eyes, preparing for the blow. My life might have flashed before my eyes if I'd had one long enough to relive.

But the blow never came.

"What's wrong?" one boy asked.

I opened my eyes and saw Chubs standing over me, holding the branch an inch from the side of my head. He raised the branch again and brought it down hard, but it stopped short.

"Hit him!"

"Shut up!" Chubs yelled. He lifted the branch once

more, but as he prepared to strike, a stone struck him above the left eye. He fell backward and let out a scream as blood dripped from his eyebrow.

One of the goons cackled. "You scream like a girl."

"Who did that?" Chubs yelled. "I'll kill you!"

That was only the second time I'd used my powers. I didn't know how I'd done it, but I could feel the stone as if I were gripping it with a phantom limb.

I pulled my arms free and twisted around since the other boys were too distracted to keep me pinned. A dozen more rocks rose from the creek bed, dripping as they hovered in the air.

"I told you this place was haunted," one kid said.

Chubs backed away from me. "Come on, let's get out of here."

The rocks hurtled toward them, and all three screamed as they turned tail and ran through the woods, dodging stones and slipping into the trees.

I waited until the coast was clear before I pushed up off the dirt.

"Come home, Cliff." It came as a whisper on the wind.

I turned, startled, but no one stood between me and the house. I walked toward it, looking for the source of the mysterious voice.

"Come home, Cliff." The front door swung open, and a swirl of darkness shot toward me, like black ink spilling over a blank page. The mass grew until it consumed the house.

I turned and ran, but the world in front of me faded.

"Come home, Cliff." The voice lingered as everything went black, and the hairs on my ears· tingled from the speaker's breath.

I AWOKE PANTING and covered in sweat. I'd had a nightmare every night since Delilah rode off in her Rolls-Royce, and most of them involved the Duncan Plantation.

Chubs didn't realize the tremendous gift he'd given me when he'd chased me down the old dirt road to the Duncans' that day.

The house was full of furniture as if the previous owners had died off or simply gotten up and left. Although water damage had rotted a good chunk of the entryway floor, the crystal chandelier still hung above the spiral staircase. The painted landscape mural that covered the walls, although chipping, was recognizable.

The place had become my personal oasis. I would spend summer afternoons reading horror novels on the second-floor balcony and watching the sun slowly dip behind the tree line, casting a vibrant orange reflection over the pond behind the house.

I didn't find joy in scaring the neighborhood kids—

well, I hadn't at first—but I had to protect my private retreat from those who came looking to break windows or, in Chub's case, break me. If kids broke in while I was around, I would slam doors and windows and fling dusty plates across the room. The secondhand ghost rumors became firsthand terrifying experiences, and none of the kids who stepped onto Duncan land during my watch ever bothered to return.

I slid my legs over the edge of the bed onto the floor, rolling my ankle as my foot landed on something sharp. A pebble had embedded itself in my heel, and I looked down at the neat pile next to the bed as I pulled it free. I rubbed my eyes so hard, it blurred my vision, but the pebbles remained. I knelt and swept the pile into my hand. My stomach churned as I ran my index finger over them and bits of dirt broke loose in my palm. They felt as if I'd pulled them straight from my dream.

"You're being ridiculous," I said to myself. "You tracked them in from the backyard." I stepped toward the bedroom door and tossed the rocks in the waste bin on my way out.

Haunting Hatchet House had lost its charm since Delilah's visit. I'd gotten sloppy with recent tours, and the day I found the pile of pebbles, I slipped in the fake blood patch and accidentally chucked a plate into the side of a tourist's head. I'd considered closing for a few days to get myself back in order, but the money was too good to pass up. Yet despite my best efforts to reason away the creeping dread slinking in from the shadows, I knew something had changed since Delilah's visit. A switch had been flipped, but I wasn't sure why.

I kept tabs on Delilah to make sure she didn't tell the world about my operations. I didn't have a computer, so I made frequent trips to the library to check the internet along with Hatchet House's email account. I'd paid a kid a few hundred bucks to build a website, and it had paid off in magnitudes.

Despite Delilah's disastrous visit, nothing popped up on the web or in my inbox, so I tried to convince myself the whole thing would blow over. Even if Delilah claimed the haunting was a hoax, any publicity was better than no publicity. Besides, she had no proof. That became my mantra. But so far, I didn't have to worry—Delilah had maintained radio silence since she'd crawled out the front door.

I walked back to the house, grabbed the mail, and tossed the junk into the bin in the entryway. As I set the rest on the phone stand by the staircase, I noticed a splatter of fake blood on the hardwood. *I must have gotten sloppy with the squeeze bottle again.*

I turned the corner and walked down the hallway to grab a rag in the kitchen then wiped up the splatters along the floor. As I stood over the sink and rang out the pseudo-bloody rag, a drop fell in front of me, and my eyes followed the wall up to the ceiling.

"Come home, Cliff," was spelled out in bloody finger paint. My heart dropped as I noticed the bloody ceiling streaks that traced a path back to the entryway.

I dropped the rag, walked down the hallway, and picked up the telephone. I'd scribbled down Val's number on the phone-stand notepad during our last call. I dialed the number on the old rotary phone and waited patiently for the wheel to whir back into place.

Val was a busy woman, so I didn't expect an answer. She had probably blocked my number after the disastrous taping.

"Hello?"

"Val?"

"Who is this?"

"It's Cliff."

"Shit," she said under her breath. "Sorry, Cliff, there's nothing I can do for you."

"Wait! Please, I'll be quick."

"What do you want?"

"I don't know what's going on, but ever since you guys left the house, my life's been a mess. I can't sleep, I'm having nightmares, and I came home today to a ceiling covered in blood."

"You don't think I'm that stu—"

"Just tell Delilah. Please. 'Come home, Cliff' was

written in blood on my ceiling. She said that same thing at the dining room table that day, and now I'm hearing it in my dreams. I keep seeing this place from my hometown, like something is calling me back there. Just tell her. If she doesn't believe me, that's fine, but if she knows how to stop it, I need to know. I'm losing my mind."

Silence filled the line.

"Please," I said.

"I can't promise anything, but I'll talk to her."

"Thank you," I replied, but she'd already hung up the phone.

I noticed the blood line extended to the second floor. My hands became cold and clammy as they slid along the stair railing. "Come home, Cliff" was scrawled repeatedly on the white ceiling.

I hadn't told Patrick about Hatchet House. I already had a lot working against me, with the whole drunk-and-disorderly act, and I didn't want to take a chance of scaring him off. The thought of explaining my powers to him made me ill, and I figured my profession as a tour guide for an infamous murder house probably wouldn't be a point in the right column either. And to tell the truth, I was embarrassed about the way I lived, holed up in a messy bedroom like a child.

Whenever Patrick and I got together, it would either be at his apartment or out somewhere. He'd asked to see my place a few times, but I'd always made an excuse. As the tours picked up, I knew it was only a matter of time before I had to come clean about my unusual profession, but had it not been for the bloody mess, I would have clung to the secret a little while longer.

But I was scared and needed help.

I pulled my old prepaid flip phone from my pocket. I couldn't risk him calling and receiving a "Hatchet House" greeting, so I never called him from the home phone. My hand shook as I scrolled through my contact list and clicked on his number.

"Hey there." His voice caught me off guard. He rarely answered the phone.

"Hey." I tried to sound casual. "Are you working tonight?"

"Nope. Free and clear. I was just about to call you. Are you home from work?"

"Yeah, you could say that." I fished for the right words. "You know how you've been begging to see my place?"

"And you've politely told me to fuck off every time. I'm starting to think you're married and have kids."

I let out a nervous laugh. "Not quite. How would you feel about seeing it tonight?"

"You're shitting me."

"No. Something happened at home, and I'm a little creeped out."

"What? Are you all right?"

"Yeah. Everything's fine... Well, it's not. But I'm okay, I mean. I need your help with something."

"What is it?"

"I have to show you. It's too much to explain over the phone." I gave Patrick the address and told him to meet me out front of Hatchet House.

While I waited for him, I climbed up on the kitchen sink with a rag and wiped off the bloody letters. Sure enough, "Come home, Cliff" was still perfectly legible even after a few minutes of vigorous scrubbing. The whole ceiling would need to be repainted. I threw the rag into the sink in frustration and walked through the house to the front porch, where I sat and waited for Patrick.

As he pulled up in his dark-blue Mazda, he rolled down his tinted window and shouted, "What are you doing here? This place is a tourist trap."

"This is my place," I shouted back, gesturing to the haunted monstrosity behind me.

He cut the engine and climbed out of the driver's seat. "You're kidding, right?"

"Afraid not," I replied as he leaned in for a hug and wrapped his arms around my waist. "I run this place."

He held me out at arm's length. "So this is why you've never had me over?"

I tried not to make eye contact. "Exactly."

"But why would you keep this from me?" he asked with a shit-eating grin.

"Because I work in an axe-murder house. I don't know. I just figured one day you might come stumbling in for a tour or that you'd just find out on your own somehow. The longer I waited, the harder it got to tell you."

"I have to admit, it's not really my type of place, but a job's a job."

"I guess you could say that."

"So what's wrong?" he asked.

I gestured for him to follow me inside.

"Wow." His eyes scanned the entryway. "This place is so cool."

"I fixed most of it up myself, but I came home from the library today and found this." I pointed up at the ceiling.

"What the hell? Is that blood?"

"Just corn syrup, fortunately. I use it for the tours."

Patrick squinted to read the sloppy text. "'Come home, Cliff.' That's freaking creepy. Someone playing a joke on you?"

"I don't know. It was probably just kids." I knew that wasn't true, but what else could it have been? Ghosts?

"Did you call the police?"

"No. I don't have time for people to go poking around. I just need help to clean it up. I tried scrubbing the ceiling, but the dye must have stained it. I have to repaint the first- and second-floor ceilings before the tour tomorrow morning."

"They got the second floor too? What assholes! Why don't you just cancel?"

"Five hundred bucks a day, that's why."

His eyes widened. "You make that much giving tours of this place?"

I nodded. "I got all the paint stuff ready. I just need some help painting."

"Five hundred bucks. Guess you're buying dinner, then."

"Of course."

For how nervous I'd been to tell Patrick, he didn't seem to care. I supposed he'd seen me at my worst and still kept coming around for some reason. An odd job wouldn't be enough to scare him away.

We covered the floor with plastic sheets and got to work. The popcorn ceilings made everything more difficult, but within a few hours, we'd erased all signs of the bloody message.

After we cleaned up, I ordered a pizza and cleared a place at the kitchen table.

"So how long have you been running this place?" he asked as he took a bite.

"Three years now. I saw it in an auction ad and knew it was the place."

"How did you find out about the murders? I've lived in this town all my life and never heard of them."

I took a bite of pizza and pretended my mouth was too full to speak as I scrambled to think of an explanation.

Patrick punched me on the shoulder. "It's all bullshit, isn't it?"

I nearly choked. "Not exactly. There are axe-murder houses." I grinned. "This just isn't one of them."

"So the whole thing is a con?"

"I don't think of it like that. This place is like a year-round haunted house. Haunted houses are fake, but people like to be scared."

"This is all so random. How did you get into haunted houses?"

"I don't know. I just have a knack for it. I started as a kid."

Patrick scrunched his eyebrows.

"Really," I replied. "I found this old plantation house when I was younger. I used to hang out there all the time. It was like my own mansion. When other kids started poking around, I convinced them it was haunted to scare them away."

"How did you do that?"

We're heading into dangerous territory. Abort!

"I'm just a good storyteller."

"Obviously if you're making five hundred dollars a day. Where do you live, though? This place looks like a museum."

"In a room upstairs. I keep it locked during the tours."

He grinned. "Show me."

I swallowed hard.

"Come on. I want to see where you actually live. You've seen my place."

"Okay, but it's like a dorm room. Don't make fun of me."

He sat back in his chair. "I would never."

I gestured for him to follow. As we climbed the main staircase, I pulled the skeleton key from my pocket.

Someone had turned my room upside down. The TV lay broken in the floor, and the bed looked as if someone had slammed it into the wall. Clothes lay strewn about the room, and pages had been ripped from my small collection of books, leaving a pile of empty spines underneath the window.

"Looks like those kids made a pit stop," Patrick said, trying to fill the uncomfortable silence.

The bedroom had been locked all day, and the window was still closed and latched. "I don't know how they would have gotten in here." I knelt next to the tattered book pile.

"Sure you don't want to call the police?" he asked.

"I'm sure."

Patrick looked down at the pile. "At least stay with me tonight. Fake axe murders are one thing, but this is real, and whoever did it doesn't seem to like you."

The drawers of my small dresser had been pulled from

the frame and tossed to the floor. I flipped a drawer over and grabbed a T-shirt from the pile underneath.

"They really made a mess of things," Patrick said.

I reached under the bed to grab my other pair of jeans. "I know. The place looks like a pigsty." Truthfully, those jeans had been under my bed for most of the month.

After stuffing an extra set of clothes into a duffel bag I had stashed in the closet, I locked the bedroom door and led Patrick to the first floor. "Thanks again for all your help."

"It's the least I can do," he replied. "But I still think we ought to call the police."

"It will be fine," I lied as I flipped off the lights in the rest of the house.

Patrick's car was meticulously clean, much like his apartment. He held the door for me as I climbed in and tossed my duffel in the back seat.

I glanced at the house through the tinted window, and it stared back at me. The bright porch lights were beacons perched against a backdrop of darkness.

I hadn't had the time to process the feelings bubbling up inside, but as we pulled away from the house, I felt a creeping sense of fear and hopelessness that I hadn't felt since I'd left home. I'd never thought of Hatchet House as my home. It was a business, a way to make a few bucks while I figured out the rest of my life. But even though I kept myself crammed into the second-floor bedroom, the place was more of a home than my real one ever had been.

"Everything all right?" Patrick asked.

I snapped to. "Yeah, I'm fine."

"You ever had kids break in like that before?"

The lie was growing tiring. "I had a few when I was fixing up the place the first year. I made the mistake of leaving the back door unlocked."

Patrick's apartment sat nestled above an office in the old town square.

"Go ahead and get out here," he said. "I'll park the car and meet you in a minute."

"Sounds good," I replied.

He pulled in front of the building and shifted his car into park. When I opened the passenger door, cold air rushed in. I'd been too anxious to notice the chill earlier, but it penetrated my flimsy hoodie with ease.

The car disappeared down the narrow alley between the buildings.

I grabbed the door handle to get out of the cold, but it needed a key. A line of call boxes sat next to it, and for a moment, I considered running my hand along the row of buttons to see if anyone would buzz me in.

I turned toward the road and looked across the square as I waited for Patrick. Water spewed from the top of the pedestal fountain in the center, the trickling sound carrying through the crisp autumn air. Soon they would shut the fountain down for winter and install the temporary ice-skating rink.

I scanned the park and spotted a figure next to a bench on the far side, standing underneath a light post. It stared in my direction, and I averted my eyes to keep from staring back. I peered around the corner, into the alley, but Patrick was still nowhere in sight.

When I looked back at the park, the figure had come closer. Now it was stationed in front of the fountain, still standing and staring.

"Can I help you?" I shouted, hoping it was some kid with nothing better to do than screw with people, but it stood unflinching.

I was scared to look away for fear the figure would once again draw closer.

"What are you staring at?" Patrick asked as he squeezed my arm.

I spun around. "Don't sneak up on me like that," I said as I pulled away.

"Sorry, I didn't mean to."

I turned back toward the park, but the figure perched in front of the fountain had disappeared. "Let's just go inside."

Patrick pulled a set of keys from his pocket and slid one into the front door. He checked his mailbox, then we climbed the stairs to his apartment and wound through a dimly lit hallway until we reached his door.

"Just a warning," he said. "I haven't had time to clean this week."

"You've seen my place," I shot back. "It looks like a crime scene."

Patrick's apartment was spartan. The door opened to a small round dining table that sat next to an efficiency kitchen. A small stack of cleaned dishes had been arranged on a towel next to the sink. A black leather IKEA couch sat in the far corner of the living room next to a floor lamp that cast a dim glow through the apartment. Unlike my room at Hatchet House, everything in Patrick's apartment looked as if it belonged and had been painstakingly kept in its proper place.

"Dirty, huh? I've got blood on the ceiling, my bedroom's torn apart, and you think your apartment is dir—"

He leaned in for a kiss. "Dirty for me," he said as he pulled back. "Mom never was much of a cleaner, so my brother and I did all the cleaning growing up. We're both neat freaks now. What time do you have to be back at the house tomorrow? We could watch a movie."

"I've got a tour bright and early, but I could probably squeeze in a movie before bed."

Patrick tossed a popcorn bag in the microwave, and we flipped through the streaming options on his TV. My head always spun at the choices. Compared to my three channels, Patrick's TV had infinite possibilities.

We settled on a horror movie, although he was typically a romantic-comedy type of guy. I was sure he'd chosen it to appease me. He tucked himself into the corner of the couch and wrapped his arm around me as I leaned against his shoulder. We hadn't had many nights together like this, and despite the events of the last few days, I felt my anxiety fading as we sat and watched the amorphous creature crawl across the screen.

I awoke in Patrick's bed—not sure how I got there—and for a moment, I forgot I'd stayed over. I reached over to the nightstand and frantically searched for my phone, which he'd set on the other side of a stack of books. I flipped it open to look at the time since the outer screen had broken ages ago.

Four o'clock. I still have at least two hours.

As I flipped my phone closed, the light from the screen cast a glow over a figure in the room's corner. I sucked in a breath as I flipped my phone back open and held it out into the darkness. A clothes hamper sat against the wall, but there were no shadowy figures to speak of.

I'm losing my mind.

CHAPTER FIVE

The footsteps started in the attic at Hatchet House a few days after the bloody message. Slow creaks in the rafters became heavy steps as the nights progressed. I pulled the folding ladder down to have a look, just in case a squatter had taken up residence above my bedroom, but found nothing more than an old storage trunk and the cardboard boxes I'd stashed there.

Most would have been terrified at the thought of a squatter in their attic, but I would have settled for an actual person over the shadowy figure that had been nipping at my heels over the last week. I could defend myself from a person. I had been mugged once, right after I'd moved to the city. The poor guy hadn't seen it coming. He'd pulled out a revolver, but before he could aim it in my direction, I sent him flying into a wrought iron fence. Moving heavy objects sapped my energy, but the ability gave me assurance that I would never have to worry about getting into a fistfight or being robbed.

Whatever was following me, though, wasn't a person. The invisible force that had been stalking me since Delilah's visit had made more frequent appearances, accompanied by recurring nightmares of the Duncan Plantation. But no matter how hard I tried to face the thing in my dreams, to see what pursued me so ruthlessly, all I found was a wall of black.

I didn't believe in ghosts. Ghosts were just something people made up to cope with unresolved pasts, but I couldn't shake Delilah's last words to me. *Something evil's following you, Cliff.*

At first, the footsteps confined themselves to the attic and only happened late at night as I teetered between the waking and the dreaming worlds. As the week went on, I would hear crunching leaves behind me as I walked down the sidewalk but turned to see no one. The days passed, and the steps drew closer as if whatever spectral force that followed me was slowly catching up. And one night, it finally made contact.

I awoke from a paranoid dream to the sound of creaking floorboards. I lay still as the thing walked the perimeter of my bed. I felt a hand trace the sheets until it stopped at my shoulder.

"Come home, Cliff." The whisper hit my ears as a pair of hands closed around my throat.

I swiped into the black, but my fists hit nothing but air. The attacker's grip tightened, and I felt its fingernails digging into my neck as it lifted me from the bed. Its grip was so tight, I couldn't swallow, and my body went into panic mode as my lungs tried to draw in air but failed.

As I began to feel light-headed, I ran my hands along the wall, frantically reaching for the light switch. My index finger grazed it, and as light rushed in, I caught a glimpse of myself in the mirror on the far wall, hanging in midair for a moment until my body fell back to the bed.

I scrambled to my feet and turned to face the room as I reached the bedroom door. I saw no evidence of a struggle or attacker except for an overturned lamp I'd kicked during the fight.

I rinsed my face in the bathroom sink and took a drink of water. My throat ached as I swallowed. I leaned in, and my heart dropped as I lifted my head. The skin around my neck was red, swollen, and sore to the touch.

I called Val and got her voice mail. The alarm clock next to the bed read 11:00 p.m.

She's on the West Coast. She should still be awake.

I hung up and tried again but got her voice mail for the second time. My message was a bit frantic.

"I know Delilah probably doesn't want to talk, but it's getting worse, Val. Whatever Delilah saw that day tried to strangle me tonight. If I don't stop it, it's going to kill me. It's got something to do with that old house I keep seeing in my dreams. It's Delilah's fault all this is happening. If she doesn't help, I'm dead, and my blood's on her hands."

I stared at my bed as my hands trembled. *No way I'm going back to sleep. What day is it? Thursday. Patrick should be at the bar.*

The chilly evening air gave me goose bumps as I power walked down the block.

"Hey, wasn't expecting to see you here," he said as I pulled up a stool.

I forced a smile. "The usual."

He seemed to realize something was wrong, raising his eyebrows as he turned to grab the bottle of whiskey and a shot glass. The bar was slammed, so he didn't bother pouring one for himself. "Everything all right?" he asked as he slid the shot across the table.

My hand trembled as I wrapped it around the shot glass. I hadn't been truly tempted to take a drink in a long time, but the attack had shaken me, and the continuous nightmares had worn down my resolve.

I lifted the glass. *Just one to take the edge off.* But before the liquid touched my lips, Patrick slapped the glass from my hand, sending the whiskey splattering onto a perturbed lesbian to my left.

"I am so sorry," Patrick said to her as he pulled a towel from his back pocket. "The next drink is on me."

I slid from the edge of the barstool, blood rushing to my cheeks.

Patrick leaned over the counter. "No, you stay right there." I hadn't seen Patrick angry before, not even with the rowdiest drunk, and the scowl on his face cut through me like a knife. He tossed the towel over his shoulder, glided to the end of the bar, and whispered to the other bartender. Then he looked at me and pointed at the front door. "Outside." It wasn't a question.

I followed him like a scolded puppy as he slipped under the counter hatch and approached the front door.

A gaggle of smokers was congregated around the bar's entrance, so he pulled me into the alleyway. "What the fuck's gotten into you?"

I swiped a trembling hand over my face. "I don't know. I can't do this anymore. It's following me everywhere I go. It attacked me tonight."

He must have seen my hands shaking under the dim light from the streetlamp because his tone softened. "Who attacked you?"

"Not who... I don't know. I think I'm losing my mind." Hot tears dripped down my cheeks despite my best effort to hold them back. I bent over and tried to catch my breath between sobs.

Patrick pulled out his cell phone and made a call. "Hey, yeah—no, everything's fine, but I need to take off early tonight. Think you could cover for me?"

A long pause followed.

"Awesome. I really appreciate it. The place is

packed, so it should be a good night." He tapped the phone and slid it back into his pocket. Then he rested his hand on my back. "I'll get you a glass of water. Come in and sit down." He reached for my hand, but I pulled away.

"No. I can't go back in like this. I'm a mess." I wiped the snot from my nose with my sleeve and rubbed my eyes. "I just need to catch my breath. I'm sorry," I sputtered. "I don't know what's wrong with me."

He nodded. "Ben will be here in fifteen, and I'll get you some water in the meantime." He ran his fingers through my hair. "Everything's going to be fine. I'll be right back." He pulled open the side door to the kitchen as I tried to pull myself together.

I tried to take a few calming breaths, but they came out short and stunted. My throat hurt with every swallow as if I'd developed a sudden case of strep.

Glass crunched at the alley entrance, and I looked up to see the figure standing in the shadows. A gust of air cut through the atmosphere, rushing toward me. I could almost see the wind as it picked up trash and scraps of paper, growing stronger as it approached. I felt the same static cling as if something were trying to pull me in and fuse with my body. The force approached in a hot blast, raised its arms, and let out a low moan that echoed against the brick walls and metal trash cans.

I opened my mouth to scream, but just as the creature's

shout became too loud to bear, a hand gripped my shoulder hard from behind.

"Jesus!" I yelled, spinning around to see what had grabbed me.

"What's wrong?" Patrick asked with a glass of water in hand.

"It's here," I said, looking down the alley. The figure had disappeared and taken the sound with it.

"What are you talking about?"

"Look." I lifted my chin and exposed the angry skin underneath.

Patrick pulled out his cell phone and flipped on the flashlight. "Who did that to you? I can see thumb prints."

"I don't know. Whoever wrote 'Come home, Cliff' on the ceiling." My cell phone buzzed in my pocket, and I pulled it out and flipped it open to check the Caller ID. "Oh, thank God," I said as Val's name flashed across the screen.

CHAPTER SIX

"A drink, sir?" The flight attendant's pin caught the light from the window as she leaned over to take my order.

God yes, please! "Just water," I replied.

"Ginger ale," Patrick said as she turned toward him.

I was shocked Patrick had agreed to come to Mississippi with me. In fact, I was shocked he was even willing to speak to me after the night in the alley. I must have seemed insane, but he'd stuck around.

I had splurged for first-class tickets. He'd insisted on paying for his, but I had refused. I would have paid for a private jet if it meant I didn't have to travel back home alone.

Delilah had agreed to bring her crew to Mississippi if I agreed to explain how I'd pulled off the Hatchet House haunt on camera. Telling the truth would ruin me—if anyone believed it—but it was worth the risk to rid myself of whatever force was following me. It would mean breaking the news to Patrick about my secret gift, and the thought made my stomach churn.

The plane crossed into Mississippi, and my gut rumbled with a mixture of fear and guilt.

Patrick rested his hand on top of mine. "You look like you're about to puke."

I swallowed hard. "I'll be fine."

"You should try some ginger ale. It'll settle your stomach." He handed me the can, and I took an obligatory sip.

"I still can't believe you grew up in Mississippi. You don't even have an accent."

"I worked hard to get rid of it," I replied. "The state can go to hell as far as I'm concerned."

"It's not exactly my dream destination, but it can't be that bad."

"You didn't grow up there." I took another swig of ginger ale. It was working.

"Was it the gay thing?" he asked.

I shrugged. "That was part of it." I was probably being too hard on the place. Mississippi was like most other states —it had good people, and it had assholes. Linwood, the town in which I'd grown up, was a different kind of rural. It was the kind that swallowed generations whole and where the few people who could escape ran like hell.

"When did you move out?" Patrick asked.

"When I was eighteen." I remembered little about my last day in Linwood. I'd woken up in my bed with a black eye, a welt, and a wicked headache. I'd decided I'd had enough of the place, so I packed a bag and left before Dad was the wiser.

"Eighteen? To go to college?"

I laughed. "Nope, no college for me. I was afraid that if I stayed, Dad would do more than punch me the next time he got angry."

Patrick grimaced. "What about your mom?"

"She left when I started middle school. Couldn't blame her either. Just wished she'd taken me and my sister with her." I looked down at my lap. "What about you? You're about to get a crash course in my shit show of a family, but you've never talked about yours. All I know is you go out to Minnesota to see your mom and brother now and then."

Patrick chuckled. "Not much to tell. Already told you my parents got divorced when I was younger. Dad moved out of state, and Mom worked all the time, so it was up to my brother and me to take care of the household stuff. She almost lost us after she hurt her back at work and developed a thing for painkillers."

"But she got over it?"

"Yeah, but that stuff's like heroine. You don't just kick it overnight. It took a long time."

"So that's why you're the neat freak, then?" I asked.

Patrick nodded. "I had no other choice. You should see

my brother. He's the wrap-your-couch-in-plastic type. Maybe you could meet him when I go home for Christmas."

"I'd like that."

The plane bounced on the tarmac as it touched down in Jackson, and we taxied to the gate. I stepped from the jetway onto the dark-blue carpet of the Jackson airport, and my feet stuck to the ground as if it were clinging to them.

"You okay?" Patrick asked.

"Fine. Let's just get our bags and go. I could use a coffee too."

We strolled through the airport and grabbed our luggage at baggage claim then made a stop at the rental car booth.

I'd worked up the nerve to drive to Dad's house before we backtracked to the motel. I figured time may have mellowed him out, and if not, I was a full-grown adult and could handle myself.

We pulled the white Civic off the road next to Dad's gravel driveway. I hadn't seen the place in years, but the memories came flooding in as I ran my hands along the steering wheel.

"We can leave anytime you want," Patrick said.

"Sure you're okay to do this? He was a drunk, raging asshole when I left. Odds are he hasn't changed much."

"I deal with drunk, raging assholes every night. I'm used to it." He squeezed my shoulder. "Let's do this."

I pulled the car down the gravel drive as the overhanging greenery scratched at the roof. I had spent most of my childhood running from bullies, running from being gay, and running from my father. His house was a reminder of all those struggles, wrapped in a dilapidated package, one I would never be able to leave behind for good.

The one-floor house sat on a concrete slab, which was in surprisingly good shape considering the flimsy structure resting atop it and the crumbling family that had once lived inside. When I lived there, the place had felt like a tinderbox—small, cramped, and just one ill-timed sentence away from bursting into flames.

The white paint on the wooden siding had peeled and cracked, exposing the wood underneath, leaving some of it weak and rotted. The driveway was empty, and weeds and overgrown grass had taken over the front bushes. A small plot of junked-out cars sat against the tree line, overtaken by weeds and brush.

"The place looks abandoned," Patrick said. "You sure he still lives here?"

"Maybe he drank himself to death." *If only.*

A shadow shifted across the newspapered window in Dad's bedroom.

I reached for the handle. "Someone's here." I swallowed hard as I forced myself out of the driver's seat. Dried leaves crunched under my feet as I crossed the overgrown front yard and ducked underneath the rusted awning hanging crookedly over the front porch.

Patrick followed closely. The glass on the screen door had been broken, and as I yanked the metal handle, a jagged shard came free and crashed to the ground.

I pounded on the interior door with my fist, and as I did, it came loose from the frame and swung open.

Patrick put his hand on my shoulder. "Seriously, if someone's camping out here, we don't want to mess with them."

I pulled away and stepped inside. No one could have been worse than Dad.

I kicked over a pair of empty beer cans as I crossed the threshold. Empty bottles, cans, and food containers were scattered about the living room. Dad's old brown armchair had been eviscerated, with torn clumps of padding scattered next to it. I could still feel the smack of leather against my ass when he would catch me with his belt if I made too much noise while he watched TV. The couch had been pushed aside, and the mattress had been pulled from Dad's bedroom and laid out on the floor. Graffiti covered the nicotine-stained walls, and someone had broken all the blades of the ceiling fan.

I flipped the switch on the wall next to me, but the

house remained dark. "They must have cut the power. I wonder how long he's been gone."

"Dunno, but it looks like someone's been using this place as a party house."

I walked down the hall to Dad's bedroom, and the carpet squished under my feet, saturated with who knew what.

"Just be careful," Patrick whispered from behind me.

I waved him away. "I'm fine." If anyone messed with me, I would fling them out the window.

I poked my head around the corner, but the figure from the window was nowhere to be found. Dad's bed frame and box spring sat in the middle of the room, and his closet door had been ripped from its hinges. Clothes lay in clumsy piles on the floor.

"They must have been looking for valuables," I said. "But all his clothes are still here, like he never left." I turned toward the room across the hall—my room. The handle was still broken where Dad had kicked it in.

"Looks like they broke this one too," Patrick said.

I didn't correct him but wiggled the handle and pressed against the door. Like Dad's bedroom, most of mine had been destroyed. I looked up at the glow stars Mom had put up for me then stepped toward the window I used to crawl out of. I could still see the edges of the raised beds where she had kept a garden in the backyard.

I turned toward the closet and shifted the folding doors

aside. The smell of mold and rot filled my nose, and I gagged as I backed away.

"What reeks?" Patrick covered his nose and stuck his head inside the closet. "That's black mold." He pointed to the top of the closet, which had been stained from water damage. "We shouldn't be in here. Looks like the roof's leaking, and this stuff is toxic."

I looked down at a decaying heap on the floor. "Oh God, it's a cat." I turned toward Patrick and gagged once more. "I've seen enough anyway. Dad's long gone. Let's go to the motel."

Patrick's lips curved into a sympathetic smile. "I'm sorry you have to see your old place like this."

"Don't be," I replied as we made our way out to the living room.

I was happy to see the place in shambles. The house had been festering for decades, and its appearance finally reflected how it had felt to live there. I was glad Dad had left. Maybe the town had chased him out, or maybe he'd found a new family to terrorize. Maybe he was dead. It didn't matter to me.

I asked Patrick to drive to the motel so I could collect myself.

"Are you getting hungry?" he asked. "It's almost two, and we haven't eaten anything since breakfast."

I felt my stomach rumble. Up to that point, I'd assumed it was just nerves. "I could go for something."

Patrick glanced at me. "I saw a diner on the way out. Wanna stop there?"

I swallowed hard. The thought of being recognized made me ill. "Can we just take it back to the motel? Don't think I'm ready to meet any of my old neighbors."

"Neighbors?" Patrick asked. "You live in the middle of nowhere."

"Townees, I mean. Everyone in Linwood knows each other. That's why I wanted to avoid it."

"Okay," he replied. "I'll get in and out, then we'll be to the motel in no time."

"We can take the main road back through town, though. I kinda want to see if anything's changed."

I took one last look at the wrecked house as the car passed and felt my muscles relax with the realization that I never had to go back there again.

Patrick rested his palm on the back of my neck as he drove. "At least the worst is over with."

I let out a nervous laugh. "We'll see about that."

"Why was your dad such an angry guy?"

I looked down at my lap. "Mom said my grandpa was really rough on him, but he died before I was born. And Dad took a pretty bad blow to the head at his job when I was younger. Not sure what happened exactly, but things went downhill after that. Mom said he was always in a lot of pain, and I think that's when the drinking started. He was just a different person after that."

"That's awful," Patrick replied.

"It is what it is."

The town was just as small as it had ever been. We entered at the far end and drove toward the diner on the opposite side. The square was still an empty parking lot even though dinner time was close and the diner was the only place to eat nearby.

Several storefronts had been boarded up, including the old comic shop that had once been my salvation from small-town life and the salon where Mom used to get her hair done. She would take my sister and me into town on Saturdays. Dad had always complained about the expense, but it was the only thing besides us kids in which Mom had taken any pleasure. The salon owner had kept a small stash of toys in the box under the bay window, and we would sit and play in the warm sun while Mom gossiped with the owner and other Saturday regulars. No signs of the once vibrant storefront remained except for a faded blue-and-white awning.

"Doing okay?" Patrick asked.

"Oh, yeah. Sorry," I replied. "The diner's just up ahead."

We passed the courthouse in the center of the square. I was uncomfortably familiar with the place by the time I'd hit my teens. At first, Dad's friendships with the local officers had been enough to get him out of trouble after they'd caught him taking a few drunken joyrides. But eventually, even the small-town justice system had caught up with him. They'd taken his license for a year, and it became my responsibility to take him on beer runs.

Patrick pulled up in front of the Silver Line Diner, but I made him move the car across the parking lot to the far side and hunched down low in the passenger seat.

Like the town church, the Silver Line had its own congregation of sorts. Amidst the boarded-up shops and shuddering small-town economy, the diner was a beacon, pulling its guests in with a spectral neon glow, silver siding, and the promise of full stomachs.

"We could just go somewhere else," he said.

"There isn't another restaurant for miles, plus they have good cheeseburgers. I'll be fine." I looked in the rearview mirror and watched him climb the steps. The blue neon lights of the diner were still as uncomfortably bright as ever.

As I waited for Patrick to return, I looked out on the row of houses across the street. A screen door opened, and a woman in a nurse's uniform emerged, led by a crotchety pug. I recognized him—Hoover. I hadn't seen the wheezing arthritic creature in years, and he hadn't aged well. He was still alive, in the strictest sense of the term, but he wobbled uncomfortably in the breeze. His joints seemed to be fused into position, and his doggy torso was so bloated, it appeared the wind could have easily carried him away like a balloon.

He belonged to Miriam, who had been old for as long as I could remember. She had been part of the Saturday morning salon gaggle, and the woman must have been in her nineties by that point.

The nurse lifted the dog, carried him down the concrete steps, and set him on the sidewalk. As he sauntered along, a sudden tapping caused me to jump.

A woman peered through the window, her brown curls pressing against the glass. "Clifford, is that you?"

I eyed the rearview, looking for any sign that Patrick was on his way, but she and I were the only two in the parking lot.

She rapped on the glass once more with her fingernails as if she hadn't been loud enough the first time.

I gave her a nervous smile and a halfhearted wave.

Patrick had taken the keys with him, or else I would have at least rolled down the window. Or more likely, I would have driven away and circled back for him later. Instead, I opened the passenger door and stepped out into the parking lot.

"It's me," I said, too taken aback by the situation to think of anything more original.

The woman stood in the glow of the evening sun, which was still too warm for the red cardigan she wore. A bead of sweat rested on her upper lip, just above her bright-red lipstick. "I was just headed to the church, and I saw you sitting there, and I thought to myself, Sue, I said, that's the Morris boy sitting over there in that car." She waited for a response as if she'd asked a question.

The jingle from the diner door gave me hope, and I turned to see Patrick approaching, holding a bag splotched with grease, a sure sign that something delicious waited inside.

Sue eyed him and smiled.

"This is Patrick," I said.

Sue tilted her head and grinned.

"My friend," I added.

Patrick shuffled uncomfortably. "Right." He held out his hand for Sue. "Nice to meet you."

As she shook his hand, I noticed that her bright-red nails matched her lipstick. "So nice to meet you." She looked back at me. "Clifford, we all thought something terrible happened to you, that maybe you had died."

"Well, I'm here and very much alive," I replied, my heart still pounding. "But we've got to get going. It was great to see you again." I crouched down into the passenger seat.

"Have you spoken to your sister lately?" she asked, not getting the hint that I was trying to get away.

"Just got off the phone with her," I lied.

"Oh, good! I'm sure she was so happy to hear from you."

"She was." I forced a smile. "Good to see you. Take care." I slowly pulled the door shut.

Sue waved and continued to stare through the window as if she'd seen a ghost.

"Let's just get to the motel." I watched Sue in the rearview mirror as we drove away. The last thing I had wanted was for someone to recognize me, and I'd made it all of ten minutes in town without being noticed.

A storm rolled in as we made our way to the motel. The windshield wipers sloshed rain off the window as we pulled into the parking lot. I'd intentionally picked a motel —the only motel—on the outskirts of town. The far end of the parking lot held a collection of rusted cars, each with prices scribbled on their windows in shoe polish, and several of the rooms had been padlocked shut.

Patrick scanned the dingy motel exterior then turned toward me. "Seriously? This place?"

"I know, I'm sorry," I replied. "I'm sure it's not that bad. Just don't want to run into a bunch of people from town."

"Your cover's blown already. How about we take the risk and rent a room where we aren't likely to get murdered?"

"Look, just do this for me, and I'll make it up to you—I promise." Before he could protest, I braced myself for the rain, pulled my jacket over my head, and hopped out of the passenger seat. I headed toward the sign that read Office, or at least I assumed it read Office. It was hard to tell since half the letters had burned out.

The office desk was dimly lit by grimy yellow lights, and dust motes puffed up from the dated floral carpet with each step I took toward reception. The clerk's eyes were trained on a small TV perched at the edge of the counter. Even the rattle of the bell against the glass door hadn't been enough to pull him from his stupor.

"Hello," I said.

He broke his gaze away from the TV screen. "Sorry." He leaned over the counter, rested his gut on the laminate countertop, and curled his lips into a wide grin. Then he reached toward the pegboard next to him, pulled a key from a wooden rung, and set it on the counter. "I'll just need a signature and a credit card, and you're all set." He pulled a sheet from under the counter and set it next to the key.

"How do you know who I am?" I asked as I leaned in to sign the form and lay my card on the table.

He pressed his glasses up the bridge of his nose and squinted. "Easy to tell when you're the only guest for the night." He twisted the paper around and read my signature. "And I thought I recognized you."

Shit.

"Clifford Morris." He stroked his chin. "We went to high school together. Don't you remember me?" He leaned back in his chair.

I legitimately did not know this man and must have done a bad job of hiding it.

"Denny," he said.

I reached for a name. I knew a Denny, but he had been as skinny as a fence post. "Bradford?" I asked.

"You remember! Say, I heard you died a few years back."

God, not this again.

"Nope, just moved," I replied.

"Oh. Maybe just the town rumor mill, then. Well, enjoy your stay. Let me know if you need anything. I'm just a short walk away."

I nodded and braced myself for the storm as I stepped outside. I inched my way along the covered walkway to our room and gestured for Patrick to pull the car around.

I slid the key into the door to our motel room, but the handle jammed as if it were trying to warn us to go back from where we'd come, that nothing good waited inside. But we'd come too far to let a crummy motel send us packing. I cranked the handle hard and rammed my shoulder into the door. Finally, the swollen wood squealed free from the frame.

The room was as expected for a roadside motel. My feet met the same floral carpet that adorned the office, and a sailboat print hung crooked on the wall as if the waves from the picture had knocked it loose. A mini CRT TV sat atop a scratched dresser, and a floor lamp cast a yellow filter over the entire room.

Patrick stepped inside. "At least the sheets are clean."

A set of bright-white sheets hung over the edge of the bed, sandwiched between an old polyester comforter and a lumpy-looking mattress. They reminded me of Denny's teeth, pearly white and oddly out of place.

"How long did you say we had to stay here?"

"The crew's setting up tomorrow morning. We'll meet them at the Duncan Plantation."

CHAPTER SEVEN

A dream brought me back to the Duncan Plantation. I turned to face the foyer. The last time I'd been inside, the house was a rotted shell, but now the warped boards in the parquet floor had been replaced and finished to a high sheen, and the entryway mural of the surrounding grounds looked freshly painted. The grand spiral staircase, once a broken and crumbling mess, wrapped around the wall and curled to the second floor, stretching to the mural's sky like a staircase to the heavens. A grand chandelier hung in the center like a radiant sun.

A creak of the floorboards upstairs caught my attention, and I approached the staircase, running my hands along the smooth handrail as I climbed. I reached the second floor and peered down the wainscoted hallway lined with rows of open doors and dimly lit wall sconces. I'd counted the rooms in the house once and had made it all the way to twenty, including all the bathrooms. But in a hallway full of open doors, the closed one at the end stood out.

I stepped down the hall, looking inside each room as I passed, searching for the source of the sound.

The bedrooms were all similar in layout, filled with cherrywood furniture and grand four-poster beds. I assumed the portraits were of family members.

I set my sights on the closed door. Flickering candle-light sneaked under the crack of the doorway. Out of all the doors in the house, I couldn't remember what waited on the other side of that one, but a feeling of dread washed over me as I gripped the handle. The floorboards squeaked once again on the other side, and the shadow of someone's feet broke the glow.

I told myself to run, but my feet refused to move. Black sludge oozed from the keyhole and slithered its way to the handle. I tried to pull away, but the sludge held my fingers firmly to the knob. My heart pounded as I twisted the knob and thrust the door open with no consideration for the person on the other side.

The room was empty, of people at least. It was just another bedroom with the same cherrywood furniture as the others. In an instant, the strange goop had vanished. I checked the corners of the room to be sure, but the only eyes watching me were those of a baby doll propped in a toy rocking chair.

I tripped on a corner of the rug as I stepped toward the center of the room and braced myself against the bed. The upturned corner revealed a stain in the hardwood. As I knelt to flip the rug back into place, I ran my finger along the wood, which was wet and spongy to the touch. I looked at the ceiling just as a droplet of water splashed on my forehead. A black stain sat juxtaposed to the crisp white plaster at the source of the drip and began to spiral outward.

A small spot had grown in the floor, causing the floorboards to warp and discolor. I stepped toward the doorway as the room aged in front of me. Water trickled down the stained walls, starting as a few drips and increasing until water poured in. The paint cracked and bubbled on the wall, and the floor itself seemed to sag in the middle.

The French doors to the second-floor balcony burst, bringing in a deluge of grungy water. Plaster cracked above me, and I stepped out of the way just in time as the ceiling crashed down and broke through the rotted wood floor. The bed went with it, and a plume of dust and debris rose from the hole like a puff of cigarette smoke as water poured in to squelch it.

I turned toward the hallway and ran. The furniture had been covered with blankets, and the carpet under my feet was soggy and splotched with mold. The steps of the spiral staircase shifted under my feet, the boards cracking and warping, causing me to panic and grab the rail to steady myself. The house crumbled around me, and more plaster fell over my head as I reached the entryway on the main level.

A person on the other side of the front door pounded violently, and I stepped back toward the staircase as water spilled over the second-floor landing. I felt the floor give way underneath my feet, and I fell through into the darkness. The pounding was everywhere.

Patrick shook me awake. "Who the hell is that?"

"Hrmfh," I slurred.

Someone knocked again on the motel room door.

Patrick rose from the bed and stepped toward the door. "Who is it?" he shouted.

"Open the damned door," someone said from the other side.

I recognized the voice and hopped up from the bed. "It's okay." I pushed past Patrick and unlatched the door.

I hadn't seen my sister in years, but she still looked as if she were waiting for the sky to fall. She locked eyes with me—red, puffy eyes framed by dark circles—and exhaled loudly as if she'd been holding her breath since I disappeared.

Her expression flickered from relief to anger and back again as she rushed toward me with outstretched arms. "Where the hell have you been? How could you run away and not call me all this time?" She buried her face in my shoulder.

I opened my mouth to speak but didn't know where to begin. "I'm sorry, Tiff." It was all I could say. I couldn't tell her the truth.

She squeezed me tighter. "I thought something terrible happened to you."

Patrick stood on the other side of the bed. The situation must have been awkward for him, but he let us have our moment.

"Come sit down." I gestured for her to take a seat on the bed and wiped the corners of my eyes.

Realizing we weren't the only two in the room, she looked at Patrick then back at me. "Who's he?"

"Sorry. This is Patrick," I said.

Tiff waved timidly and sent a smirk in my direction. "About damn time." She sniffed.

Patrick grabbed a few tissues from the bathroom and handed them to her as she sat on the bed.

"We stopped by Dad's house," I said. "The place is all run down."

Tiff looked up at me and furrowed her brow. "Cliff, Dad's gone."

"What happened to him?"

She looked down at her lap and seemed to struggle to find the right words. "He disappeared the same day you did."

"Disappeared? You mean he's been gone since I left town?"

She nodded. "Do you remember what happened that day?"

I swiped a hand down my face. "I don't know. I just remember waking up in bed. My face was bruised, and I assumed Dad had knocked me out. I'd had enough and just remember thinking that if I didn't leave, he'd end up killing me." I closed my eyes and tried to take myself back to that day, but a big black wall stood between waking up in my room that morning and the events that had led to the black eye.

"Why didn't you call me?" She scowled. "You could have stayed with me."

I rolled my eyes. "Stay with you and Bobby? Really?"

My sister had gotten out of our house the day she turned eighteen. Unfortunately, she couldn't afford rent on her own, so she'd moved in with her boyfriend, who was just as much of an abusive asshole as our father. Bobby was the reason I'd never called her after I left. She knew I hated him and that he was just as bad as Dad. I couldn't be a part of her life if she continued to make him a part of hers. But in the moment, I felt selfish. I had never stopped to consider how much she may have needed me. I'd made a terrible mistake.

She gave a smile as if she'd forgotten all about Bobby.

"You're not married to him now?" I asked.

"Bobby is long gone. Cheated on me. I got a call from the school when you stopped showing up. I went to the house, and you were gone. It looked like you just got up and left. I was worried that..."

"What? That Dad beat me to death?" I shot back.

She wiped her eyes with a tissue. "I'm sorry. I should have been there for you. I was trying so hard to get my life sorted out first. I wanted to get you out of that place, but I wound up with Bobby, and I fell into the same trap all over again."

I put my hand on her leg and squeezed. "It's okay now. I'm back, and it seems like you're doing better. Are you doing better?"

"I'm trying," she said. "I lucked into a job as a bank teller. It was like God finally looked down on me and said 'this girl needs a goddamned break.'"

I chuckled. "Is that how God talks in your head?"

She smirked. "Don't be a smart-ass."

"That's my kind of God," Patrick chimed in. "Sees somebody suffering and does something about it."

"So you haven't seen Dad?" I asked.

Tiff averted her eyes. "Not once. I went back to the house a few times, but he never came back—you never came back. Finally, I packed up what little stuff I had left over there. I think the bank might have tried to take the place back, but it's in such bad shape, they probably realized it wasn't worth the effort."

"And you didn't think to go to the police when they disappeared?" Patrick asked with an edge in his voice.

"I tried, but it's not illegal for a parent to pack up and move their kids. And you were eighteen. What were the police going to do?"

"Fair point," I replied. "How did you even find us here? Was it Sue? I ran into her outside of the diner."

"Janine, from the diner. Would you believe it—the woman's in her eighties and still works regular shifts. She saw you in the parking lot and called me."

Patrick's eyebrows shot up. "It is a small town, isn't it?"

"Everybody knows everybody. Janine told me what type of car you were in, so I took a drive this morning. There are only a handful of places to look." She paused. "You never told me what made you come back."

I'm having ghostly visions telling me to come home. I said the line a few times in my head, and it sounded almost as ridiculous as *I can move things with my mind.*

I settled for, "I've been having nightmares about home, and I thought it was time to come back."

Patrick laughed. "That's a tame way to put it."

CHAPTER EIGHT

Patrick and I slunk into a red vinyl booth at the Silver Line Diner to wait for Tiff. Half the town already knew I was there, so there was no point in hiding.

The regulars lined the linoleum counter that wrapped around the drink station. Each of them gave me the occasional stink eye as they leaned over to take bites of their senior specials.

Becky Miller, my high school principal, approached from the far end of the diner. "Clifford Morris? I heard you'd made it back to town." The woman stood a foot shorter than me and was one of the nicest women I'd ever met, but she could put a two-hundred-pound high school linebacker in his place if need be. "How are you?"

"Good," I lied as I stood to greet her.

She'd seen the worst of the abuse—the missed days, the mysterious bruises, and the slipping grades. I felt embarrassed to see her again. She knew all the family secrets.

She wrapped me in a bear hug and squeezed. "We've all been so worried about you."

The bell jingled against the diner door, and Tiff stepped inside.

Becky waved to her. "I won't keep you." She smiled. "Take care of yourself." She hugged Tiff before returning to her booth.

I bore the weight of Dad's transgressions growing up in Linwood, but with him gone, the place had lost its haze of dread and the crushing feeling that everything was just a moment away from crashing down.

Tiff leaned over the booth to hug me. "Did you order yet?" Her eyes were still red and puffy, and a rogue tear had settled in the chickenpox scar at the corner of her nose.

"Nope. Just waiting for you."

I expected Tiff to be angry with me, but aside from the initial shock, she'd shown no signs of resentment. I'd run from the town without so much as a goodbye, and for all she knew, Dad could have killed me. I hadn't visited, written, or even called to let her know I was alive. She should have been mad at me. *I* was mad at me.

Patrick got up to use the restroom.

"How long have you two been together?" she asked once he was out of earshot.

"Define *together*."

She rolled her eyes. "You know what I mean."

"I don't know. We've been dating off and on for a while. More *on* lately. He was my bartender back home." I decided to leave out the drunk bits of the story.

"Well, he's cute." She smiled. "I'm happy for you."

"I'm happy for you too. And I'm sorry I dropped off the face of the earth. I should have called you, and I feel terrible about it."

The waitress brought the coffeepot to the table and flipped Tiff's coffee cup over.

Tiff poured a splash of cream into her mug and looked down at the swirls as she stirred with a spoon.

"So are you dating anyone?" I asked.

She held up her left hand, showing off the engagement ring looped around her ring finger. "A little more than that."

"Tell me he's better than Bobby."

"He doesn't have a motorcycle like Bobby did, but he has plenty of other things going for him. He's a bank teller too, wonderfully kind, and treats me like a queen." She admired her ring as the sunlight bounced off the gems.

Patrick returned from the restroom and squeezed back into the booth. "We've got to meet the crew at the house in an hour, right?"

"The house?" Tiff looked from Patrick to me. "Dad's house?"

"No, the Duncan place," Patrick replied in between sips of coffee.

Tiff's eyes widened. "That old house you used to hang out in? Why would you go back there?"

"Long story," I replied.

Tiff reached across the table and grabbed my hand. "You shouldn't go back there. That place isn't safe."

I rolled my hand over and held hers. "I'm sure it will be fine."

Tiff bit her lip. "And what crew? What exactly have you been up to?"

I ran a hand through my hair and looked down at the scratched laminate table. I owed her the truth, as crazy as it would sound. "They're coming to film. I've been running an attraction up north, a kind of haunted house. I fooled a lot of people into thinking it was real, and before I knew it, I'd been asked to appear on one of those fake psychic TV shows. Only when the psychic showed up, she could see right through what I was doing. Ever since then, I've been dreaming of home and dreaming of the Duncan place."

Tiff's eyes darted from Patrick to me. "You shouldn't go messing around with that stuff. Someone could get hurt, especially in an old place like that. It's dangerous."

"I don't have a choice. I can't sleep. I can't work, and I feel like something is trying to kill me. I can't keep living like this. I have to go there and find out what it wants."

My sister pulled her hand away and reached for her

purse. "I have to make a call. I'll be back." She slid out of the booth, slung her purse over her shoulder, and walked toward the door.

"That went well," Patrick said with a forced smile.

Tiff returned to the booth a few minutes later. "I called off work today. I'm going with you."

CHAPTER NINE

The film crew had pushed open the rusted gate leading to the Duncan Plantation, and the metal chains and padlock lay coiled on the ground like a snake waiting to strike. My stomach churned at the thump of the tires against the slats of the wooden bridge as we crossed the creek with Tiff closely following us in her car.

I felt as if I'd stepped into another dream, like I was watching the scene unfold in third person. My father's house, for all its terrible memories, was just an empty shell, but I feared whatever waited for me behind the walls of the Duncan Plantation.

The house had collected a few extra layers of moss and grime since my last visit more than five years prior. Without my protection, front windows had been broken out, and someone had scrawled a pentagram on the front door. My chest tightened as the car drew closer, and my childhood—something I'd fought so hard to forget—came rushing back.

"You sure you want to do this?" Patrick asked as he shifted the car into Park.

"It's too late to turn back now," I replied. "Plus, it'll be nice to have a good night's sleep again. I can't remember what it's like."

Tiff braced herself against the autumn chill and tapped on the passenger window. "Are you guys getting out, or do I have to stand here and freeze?"

Patrick squeezed my hand. "If you decide you want to leave, just say the word, and we'll be out of here."

I spotted the production van parked at the side of the house. Jay and Tony were carrying lighting rigs inside.

"You know, Delilah's just in it for the fame, right?" Patrick asked. "She doesn't actually want to help you. She wants a story."

I rubbed my temples. "That may be, but as long as she fixes it, I don't care what motivates her." I was hardly the one to judge, seeing as how I'd made a fledgling career out of scaring the bejeezus out of people with a fake ghost story.

I reached for the handle of the passenger door and pulled. "Sorry," I said to Tiff as I climbed outside. "I just needed to pull myself together."

Val emerged from the doorway and waved us over.

"We still need to get a few exterior shots. Park next to the van for now."

"Figures," Patrick mumbled. "Delilah isn't even here yet."

I walked toward the front door as Patrick and Tiff moved their cars to the side of the house. I couldn't take my eyes off the place. Whatever had been calling me home wanted me at that plantation house. I could feel it in my sinking stomach.

I'd forgotten the building's eccentricities, how the tiled roof sagged in the center, and how the house had settled, forcing the front door into an odd slant that made it look as if I were standing at the entrance to a fun house. The weeds grew wild around the property, and I could barely see the edge of the pond peeking out from the tall grass around back.

"Just like you remember it?" Val asked.

"Almost. Thank you for talking Delilah into coming." I wasn't sure how to greet Val. A hug seemed too forward for someone who probably didn't like me very much, but I wanted her to know that she may very well have saved my life.

Val extended her hand. "Don't thank me. Delilah's been having nightmares too, apparently. You're lucky because that woman never changes her mind."

Patrick and Tiff rounded the corner of the house.

"I see you've brought an entourage," she said.

"Val, this is my sister, Tiff, and my boyfriend, Patrick."

Val smirked. "Nice to meet you both." She turned toward me. "We got in touch with the owner and have clearance to film as long as we need."

"The owner?" I asked. "I thought the family had abandoned the place."

Val shook her head. "The guy bought it at auction a few years back. I asked him what he planned to do with it, and he said it was on track to be demolished sometime within the next few years. He's holding out for some kind of land-development deal."

My heart sank at the thought of a wrecking ball crashing through the house.

"While they shoot the exterior, why don't we set up for the interview?"

I wasn't sure I was ready for that. "Interview, already?"

Val stepped through the threshold. "Delilah may have agreed to come, but she wants in and out as quickly as possible. We'll get all the B-roll later."

I stepped through the entryway of the Duncan Plantation house for the first time in years. The door must have been left open because the entryway floor was squishy under my feet. Other than the lighting rigs the crew had set up prior to our arrival, the place looked mostly as I remembered it aside from scattered bits of graffiti along the walls.

Several glass panels of the chandelier still hung in

place, but the others lay broken on the steps as if someone had treated the fixture like an expensive piñata.

Val stood next to a round wooden table and pulled its covering free. "I thought this would do." She ran her fingers over the table's smooth surface. "Give me a hand, would you?"

Patrick and I each grabbed a side and helped her drag it toward the lighting fixtures.

"Right here," she said.

We moved a few high-backed chairs from the dining room and pulled off their sheets.

The rusted hinges on the front door creaked as Jay stepped into the foyer. "She's on her way. Are we ready to go?"

"Ready as we'll ever be," Val replied.

A few moments later, Delilah stepped through the entryway, and the smell of stale cigarette smoke wafted in after her.

Val rushed to take Delilah's coat.

"Are we ready to roll?" Delilah asked.

"Ready," Val affirmed.

I stepped toward her. "Thanks for agreeing to meet with me."

She lurched back and held her hand up. "No, not yet. I'm not ready." She eyed Tiff and Patrick then turned toward Val. "Let's get started, then."

Unlike the production at Hatchet House, this lacked

all pageantry. No one even bothered to do my interview makeup. At first, I believed Patrick, that the filming was just another publicity stunt for Delilah, but as I watched her cross the entryway of the house and sit across from me, her expression made it clear she didn't want to be there any more than I did.

She said nothing at first and didn't even make eye contact with me as she brushed a few stray hairs from her forehead and straightened her collar. Her face was pale, and she'd tried to cover the bags under her eyes with an extra layer of concealer. But when she signaled for Tony and Jay to start recording, her demeanor changed as if a switch had been flipped. She straightened her back, crossed her hands, and tightened her sagging expression.

"So, Clifford, you claim Hatchet House is haunted by the ghosts of Henry Blumfeld and his murdered family. You've told the story to countless thrill seekers, and it's undeniable that strange things happen behind the house's walls. But you and I both know Henry's story is a complete fabrication. There's no murdered family haunting Hatchet House. So tell me how you do it, Cliff. With wireless motors? Sensors? An accomplice in the walls?"

I hadn't expected for her to jump right into it, and I felt a bead of sweat slowly making its way across a wrinkle in my forehead. Tiff knew the truth, but not Patrick, and I could just make out his silhouette standing behind the lighting rig. My pulse quickened, and my heart raced in my chest.

Delilah's stare drilled through me as I took a deep breath. "Well?"

"With my mind," I blurted out before I could stop myself.

Delilah sat back in her chair. "Your mind?"

"I can move things with my mind."

Delilah shot a glance at Val, who shrugged. "Surely you're joking."

I eyed the clipboard in Val's hand, focused on the metal clip, and tugged with my invisible grip. Val panicked and let go, leaving the clipboard dangling in midair.

Tony gasped from behind the camera, and Delilah sat frozen.

I brought it toward us and set it on the interview table. "I can move things with my mind," I said once more.

Delilah's eyes shifted rapidly between the table and Val as she contemplated her next move. "Cut the cameras."

The crew must have been in shock because no one moved.

"I said cut the goddamned cameras!" she yelled as she pushed herself up from the chair and stomped toward the front door. Val chased after her.

"Wait!" I shouted after Delilah. "I need your help!" I pushed myself up from the chair, and my eyes caught Patrick's. He stood, mouth agape, behind the lighting rig.

"I'm sorry," I said as I walked toward him. "I should have told you earlier. But how the hell do you tell someone something like that?"

His eyes flashed toward the ground. "Any way would have been better than this."

Tiff stepped in. "You mean you haven't told him?"

I flashed my sister a grimace. "You're not helping. Look, I have to catch up with Delilah before she jets off and I'm screwed." I grabbed Patrick by the arms. "Please stay with me, just for today. I promise I'll tell you whatever you want, and if you never want to see me again, I'll understand." The thought made me want to hurl, but what else could I have expected from him? I would have left me after a reveal like that.

I walked to the front door and pulled it open.

Val stood on the front porch. "Just give her a minute."

"No. Screw that." I pushed through the doorway. "Let me talk to her."

Delilah leaned against the side of the house and took a deep drag of her cigarette. "It's fine." She waved Val away.

Val sighed and slipped past me into the house.

A cigarette shook between Delilah's trembling fingers. "I don't think I can help you, Cliff."

"What? But you promised. Was it the clipboard? I'm sorry if it scared you, but you wanted the truth, and I promised to give it to you."

She flicked her cigarette onto the ground and pressed it

into the dirt with the toe of her high heel. "Look, we don't have to use the footage. You can go back to haunting houses and making boatloads of money. I'll even give the raw footage to you, and you can do whatever you want with it."

"You know I can't do that." I stepped toward her, and she slid farther down the siding. "Ever since we first met, something has been stalking me, getting closer and closer. I don't want to know what happens when it catches up, but it already damn near strangled me in my sleep."

Delilah stuck an unlit cigarette between her lips, and it bounced against them as she spoke. "And you think I've slept well? Look, I've seen a lot of weird shit, Cliff, most of it made-up nonsense, but a tiny sliver can't be explained away with tricks." She flicked the flint wheel of her lighter and held it up to the end of the cigarette.

"Then you should be able to help me," I replied.

She turned toward me, speaking between puffs. "You don't understand. Ever since we touched, I've been having dreams of this place, and it sounds like you have too."

"Yeah."

"I couldn't be sure until I felt the place for myself, but there's nothing here either."

"What do you mean?"

"This place is spiritually vacant, just like Hatchet House." She turned toward me but refused to come any closer. "Sometimes, when a traumatic death occurs, the spirit lingers. I thought that's what we were dealing with. Something bad happened in this house, something you were a part of. But if there are no forces haunting Hatchet House or the Duncan Plantation, that only leaves one other possibility."

"Yeah?"

"What you're running from is already inside you and has been for a long time, like a dormant energy. When we touched, I think it unlocked something, like our combined energy cracked a door open. And whatever's inside is feeding off you. I wasn't sure what it was at first or why that whole experience was so strange, but I can't think of any other explanation. And the telekinesis complicates things."

"Then how do I stop it?"

"We call it out like any other spirit. We open the door all the way."

"Well, what are we waiting for? You want a good night's sleep again, don't you?"

Delilah stared down into the dirt and bit her upper lip. Although she wore a thick set of armor, I was starting to see cracks.

"I've never done something like this before—houses and objects, yes, but never people. If I fail, whatever's inside could kill you and all of us by the time it's through. For a spirit to latch onto a person, well, it would have to be one pissed-off spirit. You've only gotten a taste of what it's capable of."

"But it *will* kill me if I don't do something. I have no chance if you don't help me. I'll do anything." I started to step toward her but held back. "Just tell me what I have to do."

Delilah looked up at me, her eyes sullen and tired. "We touch, like we did in Hatchet House, only this time, we don't let go."

"Let's do it, then."

Delilah stared down at the dirt for a moment. "I can't guarantee you'll walk away from this, Cliff."

"Just think of the story," I replied. "You do want a good story for your new show, don't you?"

She took one long drag off her second cigarette, flicked it to the ground, and sighed. "Let's do it before I change my mind."

CHAPTER TEN

"We all good?" Val asked as we came back inside.

"Good." Delilah's expression wasn't convincing.

Patrick and Tiff sat on a production trunk.

"What's going on?" Tiff asked.

"We'll need privacy for a moment. Will you two wait outside?" Delilah asked.

"Everything all right?" Patrick asked.

"Yeah," I lied. "We just need a minute to talk about something."

Patrick stood from the trunk. "You sure? You just told me you can move things with your mind. Not sure much else would shock me at this point."

"Cliff, tell us what's going on," Tiff said.

To tell the truth, I still wasn't sure myself. Somehow, I'd wound up haunted.

"Cliff's gotten himself into a spiritual predicament," Delilah replied. "We just need to sort it out, but the process has its risks."

Tiff's eyes darted toward me. "What risks?"

"It's for your own safety," Delilah replied. "My crew's well trained."

Tony grinned. "We've got good life insurance policies too."

Tiff's eyes glossed over.

"It'll be okay," I lied. "Nothing's going to happen to me."

"You're full of shit," Patrick said, holding his hand to his mouth. "I can tell."

"Just give us a minute." I stuck with short sentences to hide the waver in my voice.

Tiff grabbed me by the arm as tears trailed down her cheeks. "You don't get to disappear for years, not even bother to call, then show up and boss me around."

"Tiff, I—"

"No, you listen. Do you know what it feels like to think you're never going to see your brother again? To think something terrible might have happened to him? I don't care if staying puts me in danger. I'm staying, and you've got to stop with the goddamned lies." My sister may have been a foot shorter than me, but she spoke as if she were ten feet tall.

"I hate to break up the party, but we've got work to do,

so please either wait outside or get out of the way." Delilah gestured for me to join her at the table. She rolled up her sleeves and laid her arms on the table, palms upturned.

I squeezed Tiff hard.

"I love you," she said. "Be careful."

Patrick put his arm around my waist. "I'm staying too." He drew me in for a hug. "But we're going to have a long talk about keeping secrets after this."

I buried my head in his neck, and a few loose tears soaked his shirt. "I've got none left."

As Tony picked up a camera and rested it on his shoulder, Tiff and Patrick stood behind the camera crew.

"You're recording?" I asked.

"If this works, we'll want evidence," Delilah replied. "And like you said, it'll be good for the show. Now take off your belt."

"My belt?" I asked.

"You too, Jay," she added.

Jay lifted his shirt and pulled his belt loose then tossed it to her.

"What for?" I asked as I pulled my belt free from the loops of my jeans.

"We need to stay connected," Delilah replied. "If I'm to find your ghost, I'll need enough time to snoop around, and considering the last time we touched felt like sticking a fork into a wall socket, I'll need a little help keeping us together."

I sat across from Delilah and placed my hands over hers without touching her.

Jay slid the belts underneath our wrists and looped them through.

"Give me a hand, would ya?" he asked Val.

Val grabbed a belt. "Just say the word."

Delilah held my gaze. "Are you ready?"

My stomach went sour. I took a deep breath in through my nose and let it slip out between my lips. My eyes scanned the room. I'd dreamt of the house for so long, acrid dreams of rot and torment, and the thought of facing my ghoulish pursuer made me want to run. But I'd spent too much of my life running. "Ready," I replied through gritted teeth.

Delilah nodded to Jay and Val. "On the count of three, then." She gripped my forearms tightly. "One... two—"

Three came as a static shock as Jay and Val yanked the belts tight and strapped our wrists together. My ears rang, and a pulse of energy ran up my arms. For a moment, every hair on my body felt as if it were standing on end.

Delilah gritted her teeth and lurched back in her chair, but the restraints kept us firmly connected. "Why are you here?" she asked the ether. "What do you want from him?"

The table vibrated underneath us, and Jay and Val stepped back. Jay knelt to lift the second camera over his shoulder.

"Answer me!" Delilah shouted.

My heart pounded so hard, it hurt.

Delilah's expression sagged, and her head sank to the table. Her breath quickened then became labored and raspy as if she were trying to expel fluid from her lungs. "To pay the price for what he's done." Her head snapped up, and her voice echoed through the room as if the walls were shouting back.

She grinned as she leaned over the table and pulled me in close. "Long time no see, you little asshole."

I swore I recognized another face in hers, morphing together like a bubbling mess as if something wore her like a costume.

"How does it feel to be a murderer, Cliff?" the thing asked.

I yanked at the straps, trying to pull my hands free. "Help me!" I shouted.

Delilah's skin was cold and clammy, and the buckle clung to my arm like an ice cube to dry lips.

Water ran from the corners of her eyes and spewed from her mouth as she spoke. "Come, give your daddy a hug." She pulled me toward her, and I could feel the ice water running through her veins against my skin.

I wrenched my arm to the side, pulling hers along with me. I grabbed the end of the belt and pulled it loose. When our hands fell free, hers darted toward mine as I reached for the second strap and pulled.

She grabbed my wrist across the table, her fingernails digging into my skin.

I cocked my foot up and slammed it into the table. It hit her in the gut and sent her tumbling to the floor.

I rolled out of the chair as she lifted the table with one hand and flung it across the room, narrowly missing Val.

Tony dropped his camera and ran for the front door, but as he took his first step onto the porch, a force sucked him back inside. His body hit the opposing wall with a sickening thud as the door slammed behind him. "Welcome home, son." Delilah rushed toward me and reached for my throat, but her hand hung in the air as I held her back with my telekinetic grip. She pushed back so hard, my feet slid until my body pressed against the wall behind me. As her hand inched closer, Patrick barreled into her, knocking her sideways.

Delilah stumbled but quickly corrected herself, flinging Patrick off and sending him into a covered wardrobe. Glass shattered as he bounced off it and onto the floor.

Delilah stretched her hand toward the ceiling and ripped the overhead chandelier free with an invisible grip of her own then launched it at Patrick. I flung it aside just in time, and it exploded into the far wall, sending shards of glass toward Jay and Val, who broke from their frozen stances to dodge the hail. The lens on Jay's camera shattered when it hit the ground. Tiff slunk to the corner of the room.

Delilah once again set her sights on me. I hurled the two interview chairs toward her, but she knocked them aside. She grabbed my throat and lifted me into the air. "You thought you could run from me?"

I could see my father's expression clearly now, cold and unblinking. I had been with him before in this very house.

He squeezed tighter. "You can run, but I'll always find you."

Val brought a mobile lighting fixture crashing into the side of Delilah, and I fell to my feet.

I looked at the front door, which had been freed from her grip and hung limp against its sagging frame.

"Get out of here!" I shouted at Tiff. Patrick lay limp on the floor across the room. "And take him with you."

Tiff opened her mouth to protest.

"Just go!" I yelled before she had the chance to speak.

Jay and Tiff helped Patrick to his feet. I couldn't see Tony in the other room, but Val stopped midway to the door and looked in his direction. She put a hand to her mouth, shook her head, then turned toward Jay and nodded for them to leave.

Delilah brushed herself off and rose to her feet.

I looked at the spiral staircase in the foyer and thought back to my Duncan Plantation dreams. My brain tried to fill in the gaps I had somehow blocked out. I realized the truth sat in the bedroom at the end of the hallway on the second floor.

I sprinted toward the spiral staircase.

"Get back here!" Delilah screamed in my father's voice. Pieces of furniture narrowly missed me, splintering around me and crunching into the crumbling plaster walls.

Ghost powers or no, drunks have terrible aim.

Delilah growled as I reached the top of the steps, her feet thumping against them as she chased me like a wild animal. I reached the end of the hall and twisted the glass knob.

CHAPTER ELEVEN

Dad was drunk again.

He had two types of drunk: the mild kind, where he would sit out back and fall asleep in a lawn chair; and the violent kind, where his eyes went wild and anger spewed from him like water from a fire hose. His current state was definitely the latter, and I hadn't seen him so angry since the day Mom left.

To make matters worse, I made the mistake of slamming a door. He hated that. At first, I cowered in the corner of my bed as he pounded on the door from the other side. But the more he pounded, a feeling bubbled up inside me—anger.

"Let me in, you bastard!" he shouted.

I'd finally had enough of putting up with the old man's rampages. I felt the sting of every bruise he'd left on my body, and the pain became too much to bear.

I'm leaving.

I threw clothes into a duffel bag, and by the time I crawled through the bedroom window, he'd nearly ripped the door from its hinges.

I hit the gravel road, ready to make the fifteen-minute jog to my own decrepit abode, sucking in the cold autumn air along the way.

I would stay at the Duncan place for a few days to think things over and come up with a plan and a destination. Anywhere but Linwood would do, and I started to feel the weight lifting from my shoulders as I made the walk. I was free.

Dad had other plans, though.

His truck ripped through the metal gate of the Duncan place, breaking the chain in two as I raced toward the front door. He had never followed me before, but something was different this time.

I heard his voice when I reached the bridge. "Where do you think you're going?"

"Stay away from me," I shouted back as I broke into a full sprint.

The defiance must have sent him over the edge, and his boots pounded the dirt road behind me. "I'll teach you to talk back to me." He yanked my arm hard, whipping me around to face him and nearly dislocating my shoulder.

I opened my mouth to speak or cry out in pain—I didn't remember which—but he swiftly jabbed me in the eye before I could say anything. I twisted around and fell hard, my face smacking the dirt road.

My father stood over me as I rolled onto my back and brushed bits of leaves from my face. "Get your ass up and get in the truck." His eyes were bloodshot, and I could smell the booze on his breath. When I refused to move, he kicked me in the ribs. "I said get up." He turned and staggered toward the pickup.

I pushed myself up off the ground, the same earth where Chubs had nearly beaten the shit out of me with a tree branch, and I lunged. I wasn't sure why I thought it was a good idea, other than I was angry and didn't care. I hated him, and I wanted him to know it.

My father fell sideways into the truck's bumper, cracking the side of his head on the dented metal.

"Oh, shit." I wasn't sure if I said it or thought it. I'd hurt him—that much I was sure of—but it only seemed to make him angrier.

Blood poured from a gash in the side of his head as he ran his hands through his thinning hair. He stared at his bloody palm then shot me a spiteful glance, his dilated pupils looking right through me. "You trying to kill me, boy?" He grunted as he reached for my ankle, but I had better reflexes than the old drunk.

I ran, but he caught up to me at the front door. I tried to slam it shut and lock it, but he kicked it in before I had the chance. I hit the stairs and sprinted toward the door at the end of the hall.

"You're just like your goddamned mother," he shouted as he chased me down the hall and into the bedroom.

I backed toward the French doors to the balcony. I could jump into the pond and would be long gone before he came back with the truck.

"If she'd listened to me, she'd still be here. Didn't know what was good for her."

"She's better off without you," I shot back. "She's better off without us."

"She's dead, you idiot!"

His words sucked the air from the room.

"How do you know?"

He knew he'd made a mistake and let a secret into the world that was meant to stay buried. His eyes scanned the room, and he reached for a fire poker next to the fireplace.

"You did it." I felt my cheeks flush and tears form in the corners of my eyes. "You killed her."

"I didn't mean to." His expression softened for a moment, almost as if the man truly regretted it. "The bitch should have listened. You should have listened." He lifted the poker over his head.

I had never lifted a person before. Objects were straightforward—they didn't flail or fight back. Dad took extra effort. I sent him flying into the far wall, and the impact left a spiderweb-shaped crack in the plaster. He grunted and brought himself to his feet, raising the poker again. "I'll kill you, you freak." He stumbled across the room and swung before I had the chance to stop him. The poker caught me in the side of the head.

I came to as he stood over me, holding the sharp end of the fire poker against my neck, preparing to thrust it inside. Darkness crept from the corners of my vision. If I blacked out, I would never wake up again—he would make sure of it.

"You should have listened," he spat.

I spotted the wardrobe in the corner of the room. With my last bit of strength, I grabbed it with my telekinetic grip and pulled.

My father turned his head just in time to see the wardrobe flying toward him. It struck him like a speeding freight train and drilled him into the French doors, which exploded in a shower of splintered wood and glass.

I rolled over onto my stomach and crawled toward the balcony. Between the blows to my head and tossing heavy objects around the room, I'd sapped all my energy. I could have slept for a decade, but first I had to make sure I would be able to do so safely.

My father had gone over the railing and into the pond —that much I could tell. I pulled myself up against the metal railing and peeked over the edge. The wardrobe must have fallen on top of him. I stayed just long enough to see that he hadn't risen from the depths and managed to make it to the front porch before the darkness took me too.

CHAPTER TWELVE

Weather had seeped through the broken French
doors, corroding and spoiling everything inside. I
stepped toward the splintered doors I'd sent my father
through years prior and onto the narrow balcony.

"I killed him," I said under my breath as if it were still a
secret.

The air was crisp—I'd been too busy to notice before—
and the chill sent goose bumps up my arms. I took a deep
breath. I was free from the secret my subconscious had
hidden away from me—a secret only Delilah had been able
to pry from the recesses of my mind.

Banging on the door behind me pulled me from my
daze.

I wasn't sure why I'd locked the bedroom door. I knew
it wouldn't stop him.

The door shot open, and bits of doorframe flew in all

directions. The floorboards creaked as Delilah crept toward me. My dad was coming to finish the job he'd started years ago.

I waited until I felt her breath tickling the hairs on the back of my neck and turned to face her. Instead of waiting for her to attack, I lunged and tackled her to the ground. She grinned wide and pushed me away with such force that I left the ground completely. But I had abilities of my own, and as I fell to the floor, I reached for her with my invisible grip and pinned her down.

I felt my father squirming at the edges of her body, his ghoulish phantom limbs struggling to escape my grip. I wrapped my telekinetic hands around him and pulled. If I was going to die, I would be sure to take him with me.

The hairs on my arms stood on end as I wrenched my father free from Delilah's body. At first, I thought I'd killed her, but she let out a soft groan as she lay on the stained hardwood floor.

My father was a misty specter dangling against the backdrop of the rotted wood and mold.

I stepped through the broken French doors and onto the balcony. It hurt to hold him, and every muscle in my body ached as I gripped his spirit tight. I stepped toward the ledge and held him over. "I remember. That's what you wanted, isn't it? But I'm no murderer. You're the murderer."

He was afraid. He'd always been afraid, and as I held

him over the murky water, I felt the bond between us breaking.

"I may have to live with what I've done, but I don't have to live with you anymore. You have no power over me." I put one foot over the railing then lifted the other until my feet rested on the edge of the roof. I wove my arms around the wrought iron and took a deep breath.

I'll send you back where you belong.

I leaned forward, and the breeze rushed against my face as my feet left the edge. My father tried to pull free, but I gripped even tighter. The pond rushed toward us. I wondered if his body was still down there, waiting.

My body broke the surface, and my muscles tensed in the frigid water. I hung in the filthy water, rays of sunlight barely penetrating the surface as I sank deeper into the abyss, pulling Dad's spirit with me.

But as the air left my lungs, another force seemed to have taken over, pulling him away and deeper into the black.

He tried to hold on, to pull himself back inside me, but with all my remaining strength, I shoved him down as hard as I could until I couldn't feel him anymore.

A splash came from above, and a hand frantically gripped mine, trying to pull me to the surface. For a moment, I wanted to stay there and sink down into the silt and debris of my past.

The hand persisted, though, grabbing for my shirt and

yanking me toward the surface. I fought, but whoever was pulling me from the depths brought reinforcements. They dragged me toward the bank, and multiple sets of hands clung to me as they pulled me onto land.

Tiff leaned over me, soaking wet, as I sputtered and coughed. Val and Patrick stood next to her as Jay barked details frantically into his cell phone.

"Just snapped Tony like a fucking twig," he said.

I rolled to my stomach and let out another mouthful of water.

"Are you okay?" Tiff asked.

"I'm fine," I replied. "Delilah's still inside. Make sure she's okay."

I sucked in fresh air and tried to catch my breath as if I'd been running since birth.

CHAPTER THIRTEEN

*O*bservation was code for "we'll let you leave when we feel like it." But I had no hopes of seeing the free world anytime soon.

I repositioned my body in the hospital bed to squelch the dull ache running up my spine. Patrick had fallen asleep in the chair next to me, and his hand lay limp on the edge of the bed. I reached over and squeezed it tight.

The shroud obscuring the details of my last day at the Duncan Plantation had been pulled away, and memories ran through my head on an unending loop.

My sister appeared in the doorway and gave a meek wave as she crossed the room. "The sheriff wants to know if now is a good time to talk."

A uniformed man appeared behind her.

"As good a time as any," I replied. "I've got nowhere to be for the foreseeable future."

Patrick sat up in the chair and wiped the corner of his mouth.

"Can you give me and Cliff a minute?" the sheriff asked, gesturing in my direction.

Tiff nodded and motioned for Patrick to follow her into the hallway.

The sheriff pulled the chair Patrick had been sleeping in around to face me.

I'd seen the sheriff around town before, and I was sure he knew me, or at least knew our family from all my dad's run-ins with the law. A wave of embarrassment radiated from my stomach.

"Son, you want to explain to me why I've got a body that's been snapped in half lying in my morgue right now?"

Tony.

"I—"

"I mean, I've seen the goddamned footage from the camera, and I still can't make heads or tails of it. I've done a handful of interviews at this point that all say a ghost did it, and I've got nothing to prove them wrong. What the hell happened in there?"

"They're right," I replied. "If the footage shows it, then you have your answer."

He put his head in his hands and massaged his temples. "You've had one hell of a day, haven't you, Cliff?"

I chuckled.

"Got to say, I'd hoped if you ever came back to town, it would be under better circumstances."

I smirked. "I've got big shoes to fill, sir. Have to live up to the family name."

The sheriff lifted his head. "What do you mean?"

"I killed my father, sheriff. I pushed him into the pond from the second-floor balcony at the Duncan place a few years ago."

The sheriff's chin stubble sounded like Velcro as he scratched it. "Over the balcony?"

I nodded. "You found the body, didn't you?"

"Yeah."

"Then what more do you need to know? I watched him go under, and he never came back up. I killed him."

The sheriff removed his hat and leaned in. "Look, I know your daddy put you and your sister through hell—the whole town knows it. If you pushed him over, the fool probably deserved it. If you want to keep thinking you killed him, that's your burden to bear, but as far as I'm concerned, the bastard had it coming."

"But I *did* kill him."

"Why'd you push your daddy into that lake, son?"

"He was chasing me, trying to kill me."

"And you defended yourself." It wasn't a question.

"I—"

"You defended yourself. No jury in the world would convict a kid whose daddy beat the shit out of him on a regular basis. So I recommend you let it be and move on."

I didn't know what to say. "Thank you," was all I could manage.

The sheriff put his hat back on. "Anything else you wanna come clean about?"

My memory flashed to Dad standing over me with the fire poker.

"Not me," I said.

"'Scuse me?"

"My dad said he killed her, sheriff. He killed my mom."

The sheriff leaned back in his chair. "You sure 'bout that?"

"He said she ran out on us. I should have known it was all bullshit. That son of a bitch killed her."

The sheriff's eyes flashed to the doorway, where Tiff stood frozen, holding a can of soda.

"What?" she asked, her voice quivering.

"Oh God, Tiff, I'm sorry. He said it when we were on the second floor of the Duncan place. He let it slip and was going to kill me to cover it up, so I stopped him."

Tears streamed down Tiff's face as she crossed the room and sat next to me on the bed.

The sheriff put his finger to his lips. "I'm going to give you two a minute. I've gotta make a few phone calls."

Tiff leaned in and wrapped her arms around me.

"I'm sorry, Tiff. I didn't want you to find out this way. I was going to tell you once this had all settled down."

"I—" She tried to speak but only managed a sob.

"What is it?"

"I haven't been honest with you," she replied in a whisper.

"What do you mean?"

She sat up on the bed, her face red and puffy. "You really don't remember how you got back to the house, do you?"

I shook my head.

"I got a call that day from the school. They told me you'd missed again. I couldn't shake it, the feeling that something bad had happened, and I left work to go find you. Dad's truck was gone. I knew he didn't go to work until late. I knew how much you liked spending time at the Duncan place, so I drove by and saw his truck next to the house. I saw you lying on the front porch. You murmured something about killing Dad. I was so afraid for you, afraid of what would happen if the police found out. So I helped you into Dad's truck, got you to your bedroom, then parked it out in the woods behind all his junked cars. I walked back to get my car, and by the time I got back to the house, you were gone."

* * *

THE POLICE SWEPT Dad's property and found our mother's body beneath a junk pile in the backyard. The bastard had barely dug a grave deep enough to hide her.

It hurt to think she'd been so close for all those years, watching over us from only a few dozen feet away. The guilt of killing my father passed quickly, but the guilt I had for believing our mom had abandoned us would linger for years.

I left my father's ghost at the bottom of the Duncan pond that day along with the powers I'd used to put him there. I tried to continue the haunt, but without my powers, Hatchet House lost its allure with the clientele. I didn't mind, though. It was time to move on. Ever since I'd encountered a real ghost, I lost all enthusiasm for pretending to be one.

I grabbed the stack of mail from the mailbox then turned to head inside. I'd filled in the post holes where the Hatchet House sign had been, and the grass seed was finally starting to sprout a vibrant patch of green. I'd rolled over the house's crusty yellow paint with a fresh coat of grayish blue and repainted the trim a bright white.

I took the sidewalk to the front steps and stopped to admire my house. *The old girl looks pretty good.* I'd used some of the tour money I'd saved to spruce the place up, and I'd even replaced the rotted boards on the front porch.

When Hatchet House closed, I'd moved out of the small bedroom and into the master. I'd also disposed of the

Blumfelds' belongings—I was sure they wouldn't mind. Although I had technically lived in Hatchet House for several years, the place finally started to feel like home.

Patrick got me a job as a barback for a few weeks until Tiff's call to the local branch of her bank netted me a teller position. I'd squirreled enough money away from the tours to float for a while and wasn't desperate for cash, but the job gave me direction and a way to fill my time.

I flipped through a few credit card offers and marketing mailers until I came to the tan package underneath.

"Anything good?" Patrick asked from the living room. In the weeks following the incident at the Duncan Plantation, Patrick had been instrumental in transforming Hatchet House, and I'd asked him to move in once his apartment lease was up.

"Mostly junk," I replied as I ran my finger along the edge of the padded envelope.

I opened it and pulled a DVD case free along with a handwritten note and a legal-looking document.

Cliff,

Can't say I've been eager to speak to you, so I hope you won't find me contacting you by letter offensive. Enclosed is the rough cut of the Duncan

Plantation episode. Considering the circumstances,
I've given you final say over whether the episode
airs. Look at it, and if you'd like to move forward,
please sign the enclosed document and mail it
back. It'll go up with the full series in a few
months.

For what it's worth, it's the strongest episode in
the series. We have very few documented cases of
paranormal phenomena with this level of evidence.
The world needs to know that there's something
after death, anything. I know your father was a bad
man, but this case could help a lot of people, Cliff.

Hope all is well and your sleepless nights have
ended. If you ever need anything, please give Val a
call.

Delilah

"WHATCHA' got there?" Patrick asked as I rounded the corner into the living room.

"Just a video. Want to watch?"

ENJOY THE BOOK?

Check Out Chris Cooper's Other Books

House of Sage and Salt

The Dreadful Objects

The Oliver Crum Trilogy

Please Consider Leaving a Review

Reviews help tremendously. Please consider leaving a review on Amazon or Goodreads!

Want to Stay in Touch?

Visit Dreadfulmedia.com to join our mailing list, report errors, or just say hello.

ABOUT THE AUTHOR

Chris Cooper is a writer, college professor, novice coffee roaster, and recovering engineer. He lived and worked in Japan, where he developed an obscure obsession for fancy fountain pens and currently lives in Ohio with his partner and Australian Cattle Terrier. Both enjoy going for walks. Chris writes horror and supernatural thrillers full of colorful three-dimensional characters, macabre adventures, and twisty turny plots.